Struggles & Strikeouts: You're Up!

by
J. Burns Alston

 www.trafford.com

North America & international
toll-free: 1 888 232 4444 (USA & Canada)
phone: 250 383 6864 ♦ fax: 812 355 4082

Dedicated To...

Thank you to all who helped me in any way – from the cover to the final word. Also, to my many caregivers who went through this with me and to those who struggle in life and that's everyone!

"*It is now 5 A.M. and since 2:30 this morning, sleep has gone somewhere! Maybe I'm getting older? No, that can't be,*" I smile pulling my body up and out of bed. "*Guess I may as well hen peck away on the computer for awhile,*" I think to myself staggering down our carpeted hallway and no I'm not drunk! I muse, "*I'd like to share some things I've learned over the past sleepless night and several year course of an illness my family and I all share. One thing I have certainly learned is that life is really not about me all that much. Life is mostly about those we love and care about - others. I hope these writings help you better understand your own struggles and strikeouts and help you appreciate even more those in life you love. They sure have helped me! There's something about writing, even on a computer, which clarifies my thoughts.*"

Chuckling to myself I recall a recent Hagar the Horrible cartoon. Hagar says to God, in essence, "*I work hard, but something always puts me down. Life isn't fair!*" Hagar then out of frustration looks up to God who replies to Hagar, "*You're just finding that out?*"

About This Book

Within these pages we will look at the relatively untalked-about, all-to-often-avoided, but much needed-to-be-understood doctrine of suffering!

You may think, *"Well, I'm okay because I'm not suffering right now,"* but you would be unwise. Not to be pessimistic, but try as we might, eventually, all people must suffer in some way. Ignoring this reality certainly will not make it just 'go away'.

In the game of baseball the entire object is to reach home safely. Reaching our heavenly home safely is also our goal in living as well - at least I think it should be.

My hope is that this book will better help you make some sense of your life and suffering too - help you have *"eyes to see and ears that hear"* (Jeremiah 5:21).

Philosophizing about life probably drives my family crazy sometimes. Oh well!

Philosophers and common people alike once believed our globe to be flat, but today, we know this is not so. We have changed our way of seeing the world – philosophizing can do this!

In today's high-tech world where a person is almost expected to spend their time digesting T.V. with its many commercials, fighting congested traffic, and listening to rock and roll on your I-Pod etcetera while trying to drive, I think reading a good book, which can positively effect your future thinking, is well worthwhile. Reading can also be entertaining and an alternate view of our world can slow the pace of life down just a bit and help you make better sense of your life.

Life can be hard! Here I offer you some encouragement and comfort.

Of suffering the apostle Paul writes in our Bible, *"For I reckon that the sufferings of this present time are not worthy to be compared with the glory which shall be revealed..."* (Romans 8:18)

All believers of the Bible take great hope in these words! Paul continues, *"But if we hope for that we see not, then do we with patience wait for it."* (Romans 8:25)

I decided I wanted to write about suffering.

My reading has just included Sidney Poitier's autobiography in which he himself begins by saying he felt 'called' to write his history. I too have felt called to write this manuscript about human challenges.

Of course I value virtues such as integrity, forgiveness, and simplicity, but in life since we all suffer at one time or another I feel the world can best use these thoughts on pain and patience.

The prophet Daniel speaks of a time to come upon this earth and warns us, *"...there shall be a time of trouble, such as never was since there was a nation..."* (Daniel 12:1)

This time must come, but the good need not fear for I believe Daniel's other words as well. Christ's second coming will be a "great" day for the 'good' and a "dreadful" day for only the 'bad'.

The Lord promises something comforting in Matthew's seventh chapter. He says, *"Therefore whoever heareth...and doeth.... I will liken unto a wise man, which built his house upon a rock. And the rain descended, and the floods came, and the winds blew (a time of trial and struggle came), and beat upon that house; and it fell not: for it was founded upon a rock."* (Matthew 7:24,25 – words added) In this parable notice that winds (trials) struck both houses – the one built upon a rock as well as the houses (lives) built upon the sand!

It is my unalterable belief that in life we all must endure something, some time, which goes down pretty hard. I remember in my childhood being sometimes presented with rutabagas to eat. A wise mother left the consumption of this veggie to her son. Have you ever eaten a rutabaga? I pride myself on being a pretty good speller, but I think rutabaga's correct spelling should be rude-a-beggar. Some people can handle them, but to me they are a rude beggar. If you ask me, they even stink! I ate them, but I never much liked them.

I am a very blessed person! Sure, I have a slowly degenerative brain disease (ataxia) that doctors say will shorten my life here; eventually make me spastic, and the medical community has yet to discover a cure for this illness, but that's life!

A well-known actor many people know has Parkinson's disease. He says of himself, *"I'm a lucky man."* Some days I agree - except for the 'lucky' part! About 'lucky' I'm not sure.

If you are reading this, you have been given time to consider life and prepare to meet God, so at least in that sense you are blessed. Come to think of it, we all ought to be getting ready to meet God.

I have always felt there are few coincidences in life – things happen for a reason!

I first thought of naming this book, **"Life as a Spaz!"**, but friends and family felt otherwise. Also, since we've all at one time or another had someone say to us, **"Life's not fair!"** and because I love the symbolism found within baseball I decided on the title **"Struggles & Strikeouts: You're Up!"**

We all take turns 'at bat' facing various struggles and baseball helped me understand some of life's lessons.

This is the second book of what is called my **"Running On Empty?"** series.

In the first book entitled **"Running On Empty? A Practical Guide to a Contented Life"** I explained behaviors needed to 'fill up your tank' and get yourself on a peaceful path. In **"Struggles & Strikeouts: You're Up!"** I try to explain what you can do when you have an 'accident' while on that pathway.

People all over this globe falsely believe that if they just do as God says, they will prosper financially and have few challenges. I don't believe this – neither does Hagar – anymore!

If people have read the Bible, some do not understand it! The Lord does not promise that our lives will be trouble free, but rather, that amidst our troubles we can find some peace. Adam and Eve suffered through one son murdering another, Moses' life was threatened and his own parents had to 'abandon' him to a stranger – Pharaoh's Princess, Joseph's life was threatened and then he was thrown in a pit and sold into slavery by his own brothers, but all of these individuals overcame their difficulties. Maybe we can learn from them?

I am not much concerned about your color, your beliefs, or where you come from. We are all human beings and as such share much! One commonality is that we all must suffer to become strong and more like God!

You need to know that I benefit by writing this book as much or more than you do by your reading. It's kind of like giving a public speech – the number one benefactor is yourself!

As mentioned, this book tries to make some sense of our suffering. Suffering often may even seem undeserved.

Few of us will struggle as much as the Apostle Paul to whom the Lord gave, not a rose, but a thorn. *"...there was given to me a thorn in the flesh."* And why was righteous Paul given his 'prickly thorns?' Paul, himself, said, *"...lest I should be exalted above measure"* (2 Corinthians 12:7).

Paul's life wasn't easy. *"Of the Jews five times I received forty stripes less one. Thrice was I beaten...once was I stoned, thrice I suffered shipwreck, a night and a day have I been in the deep...in perils of waters, in perils of robbers, in perils by mine own countrymen...in perils among false brethren; In weariness and painfulness...in hunger and thirst, in fasting often, in cold and nakedness* (2 Corinthians 12:24-27).

It seems like some people cope better with trials than others. Why is that? The answer lays somewhere in hope and trust.

Challenges, if we allow, unleash our abilities to become more loving, faith-full, and patient. In the end – more like Jesus Christ. This kind of makes one wonder if having challenges is **all** a bad thing.

Don't you find it just a bit irrational to say we want to be like Jesus, but never pass through anything remotely similar?

I'm not too sure who 'they' are, but they say, *"Life is hard and then you die and in between you're a volunteer."*

This is a book to be contemplated when things in your life or around you are unusually difficult – when you or a friend or family member suffers – often seemingly 'unfairly'.

Throughout the course of this book, I have <u>underlined</u> what helps me cope with life and also may bring a measure of comfort to you. <u>The reader will benefit most when underlined teachings are read and implemented and some personal thinking and writing is done too.</u>

I have read excellent pamphlets on suffering, but never an entire book? They are few and far between – the books I mean – not the struggles!

These thoughts will also help prepare you for tough times in your own life, which must inevitably come your way. Sadly, difficulty even strikes some in their youth. We will all suffer (though we might not want to think about it) and only our trials and how we cope will vary.

I don't want to be the harbinger of 'bad' news, but sometimes we, or someone we care for, will get sick, lose a job, lose a spouse, suffer depression and it's dark thoughts, or become addicted etc. In these pages I address many human sufferings and offer to all a portion of the healing 'Balm of Gilead' (Jeremiah 8:22).

I don't know all the answers, but could God stop our suffering? Yes, God could end our pains, but the truth is suffering is part of a loving plan. Seems strange, I know!

My aim is to leave you with a 'forever perspective'; to help you make some sense of your pains, and find help even now! I will cause you to view difficulty differently – *for as a man thinketh*...

It is the preacher, Norman Vincent Peale, who is often credited with first saying that when you change your thoughts you can also change your world.

It seems there is no shortage of suffering in our world! No matter what religion we are or how 'good' we are, we all encounter pain. However, to suffer 'meaninglessly' is not necessary!

One snowy October morning a young couple buried their three-month-old son. Our exit routes and life's timing certainly vary. How do you and your beliefs explain a child's death?

Often, we simply ignore these harsh realities. Or, all too often people, both purposely and unintentionally, have accepted falsehoods as truths.

For example, I recall a Sunday Schoolteacher who once innocently taught me incorrectly that repentance was like pulling a nail out of a board. You may remove the nail, but there will always be the mark. Truth is, God says of forsaken mistakes, he'll remember them no more. There will be no 'mark'!

Live life now like you were dying – surprise - you are!

This book presents a theology for the average person – a theology of hope and of purpose!

Especially true in our times of trial is, *"The fear (respect) of the Lord is the beginning of wisdom..."* (Proverbs 9:10).

About The Author

I like to think of myself as a bit of a modern-day philosopher. I don't say this in any egotistical way; I simply enjoy writing about everyday things like baseball and comparing them to life. I am a practical writer not a literary or a poetic one.

I won't say much about myself or of credentials because I am not that important to most people even though my mom, wife, children, and siblings would hopefully disagree.

Long ago I learned that really it is plain, simple people and the truth that matters the most in life.

Of the greatest men and women ever to have lived, scripture simply says, *"And they died..."* and then we turn the page of history.

Let me say that my immediate family and I know a bit about struggles and strikeouts and we know that we are certainly not alone.

Even though you and I are 'children of God' from experiences in life I have concluded that God does not need a 'wretched' you or me. The Lord would have us trust Him and be content in the midst of our trials.

Regardless of our struggles and strikeouts God does care for us. We are blessed just to be alive! There has never been a time in life where deep down I did not know of a God and of His love for **all** of His children.

There have been times when I have felt a bit Job–like - picked on - but I have always believed.

Job said it this way, *"Though he slay me, yet will I trust in him..."* (Job 13:15).

It seems the epitome of egotism not to think that there is a power higher than poor, pitiful me. What even gives mankind the right to doubt God even if things seem to go very 'wrong'?

I did all the usual things an average 'good' boy does like going to university, finding and holding down a job, marrying, and raising some wonderful children for which I will be forever grateful. Yet, in my late forties (I know that seems old to some of you, but it isn't really) I contracted a rare neurological illness, which quickly changed our lives, as we had formerly known them. Now I tell my wife, Karen, *"We* **are** *the service project!"*

I find that faith has a lot to do with any current or future state. I don't know about you, but my mom taught me some religion. She used to say things like, *"You better pray that will come out of my new carpet!"*

All joking aside, from Dad and Mom's teachings (thank heaven for them) I went on to fulfill many Christian responsibilities.

Some say they can't understand why such a thing as sickness would befall us.

Somewhat dumbfounded by what had occurred in his own life, King David once asked God, *"...Doth thine anger (even) smoke against the sheep of thy pasture?"* (Psalm 74:1, word added).

"Yes, no matter who we are or how well we try to obey God, we all suffer and have our Goliaths to slay, but a challenge also gives one a sharpened perspective on life and God. You begin to see what others may not. Join me as I share some of the things I, and numerous others, have learned as we have experienced this vital change of perspective."

Contents

Prologue

D id you ever notice that the word 'life' contains the word 'if'? Well, it does and life does have its share of ifs. **What if** I, or someone I care deeply for, get very sick? **What if** there is an accident? **What if** someone is suffering from some strained relationships? **What if? ...** and the list goes on! Yes, there are many ways people can suffer, but currently suffering or not, remember that life goes on.

It was an ideal day for a game of scrub baseball as a crowd of local, unsupervised kids formed at the SW baseball diamond early Saturday morning.

Today, my team would be playing against some other local kids and as usual two of the most popular locals stepped forward and one future team captain (hopefully for the other team) tossed a wooden bat to my future team's captain, which he caught with his bare hand. From this point on it was dirty hand over dirty hand to see who'd pick players first and then begin the batting. The person last able to hold the bat up in the air by its knob wins.

As in some days in life, my team won that day, but as in life too, someone had to 'lose'.

So, people have told you that *life's not fair?* Well, in a way they're right – things in this world do appear very unjust at a quick, passing glance.

The young die. A five year old was excited to start kindergarten, but instead, she recently passed away with family left to mourn. Children and relatively innocent adults suffer through divorce, they get sick, others are alone, and some appear to be born 'less than perfect'.

Even Christ's mother, Mary, was told by Simeon while presenting her Son at the temple that, *"...a sword shall pierce through thy own soul..."* (Luke 2:35). This was surely true as Christ and His loved ones bore His crosses.

My elder sister once compared the 'natural man' battle within us to having two beasts inside. The beast that wins the fight will **always** be the one we choose to feed – always! So, even when life doesn't seem fair, let's feed the right beast.

Billy Graham's wife reportedly once said something like this, that, *"God never promised an easy trip, just a smooth landing."*

Since encountering some of my own pain, I have read and re-read the Bible's book of Job. Here was a man who knew pain.

In my opinion, all who try to alleviate people's pain would do well to follow Job's example, *"...I delivered the poor that cried, and the fatherless, and him that had none to help him. The blessing of him that was ready to perish came upon me: and I caused the widow's heart to sing for joy...I was eyes to the blind, and feet was I to the lame. I was a father to the poor: and the cause I knew not I searched out"* (Job 29:12-16). Job really was a perfect man, yet despite all the good works Job performed, he had to suffer and lost it all for a while.

You might also enjoy reading Psalms number 23, which informs us that even if our struggles take us for a, *"walk through the valley of the shadow of death..."* we need not fear. God is nearby and his rod (a symbol for His word) and His staff (a symbol for His power) will bring us a measure of comfort.

I believe that in the end all will be more than fair, but it takes trust – an unshakeable hope in some things you may never see in this lifetime!

Some say seeing is believing, but I have found that believing is seeing.

I don't know about you, but I don't want what I deserve when I die – I want and envision – even expect - more!

The Apostle John, who knew Christ personally as a friend, suffered in jail on the Isle of Patmos (Revelation 1:17). John knew we'd suffer too so he counseled us, *"Fear none of those things which thou shalt suffer..."* (Revelation 2:10).

The other day I was sitting (I do this a lot now-a-days) listening to a radio talk show. The caller was complaining to a well-known female doctor of psychology about the caller's seemingly unfair lot in life. During this interview, the caller inadvertently mentioned her three children. The doctor then asked her an interesting question. *"How much more does God need to bless you before you'll recognize the good in your life?"*

Heaven knows we'd change a few things if we could! But, if we are not wise we may simply buy into the saying, *"Life's just not fair!"*

Difficulty, hard as it may be, has its purpose. The problem is we view difficulty as just that – difficulty only. We do all in our power to avoid trouble and we should, but the truth is, challenges will eventually find each of us anyway.

If you read my first book you came to realize that we too often allow life to become overly busy and unfocused. We must first get on the correct path (for me this is the Bible's path), and I believe that all good things are on that path!

From this first book I hope the reader-received direction, but never did the author mean to imply that he understood all of life's challenges completely. Few do understand life fully.

"Struggles & Strikeouts: You're Up!" will help sharpen your life-vision at an almost unbearable time of hardship – and that's a promise!

There are no pat, simple answers for all of life's struggles. But...

The Bible says Job was a 'perfect' man and yet, as before mentioned, he 'lost it all' for a while. Perhaps you feel like Job. *"Behold, thou hast instructed many, and thou hast strengthened the weak hands. But now it is come upon thee, and thou faintest; it toucheth thee, and thou art troubled" (Job 4:3-5).*

We all face crises in life. Another good Christian man I personally know well, contracted Parkinson's disease. I will never forget his final pulpit speech where he assured us his disease had its advantages. He then told us that, *"When his wife asked him to shake something, there was no problem!"* We laughed and cried together.

In life we all get 'shaken' from time to time. Yet, our pain is not without purpose! We'd be wise to come to the realization that we can, and often must, at least slightly alter our course for a time.

For example, since our disease we have a list of 'advantages' of our trial, which I will share along the way.

Sometimes confusion of one's theology can cause as much suffering as your particular challenge or challenges! These writings will help you better understand the theology of God and pain.

Be sure to follow your heart when it comes to your beliefs. Remember, correct beliefs should make some sense of life for you.

If confused on truth about suffering, this book is a must read.

I long ago decided that the acidic emotion of self-pity never gets you anywhere worth traveling.

As a former elementary school teacher I was familiar with the saying, *"Life's like a test."* It's true! In this book we have the opportunity to work together and not only share this exam, but actually be more confident in our responses. Now, let's pass!

Post Prologue

(Hmm! Never seen one of these before.) If there is one word in the English language, which I dislike most it is the word 'I'. However, at the suggestion of a dear friend I will write this book, which includes what my family, an ordinary family, are presently passing through. Because we are now passing through our own difficulties, this will allow the true teacher in me to speak from the heart and hopefully add some authenticity to my words.

I believe that sometimes very well disguised 'good' can be found even while enduring an affliction – at first you likely do not see it, but it's there! We are unwise to just 'give battle' to our troubles. We are wise when we focus on the 'pluses'! After all we must die sometime.

In a day when it seems the unaccomplished, everyday person can become famous; I guess I dare use 'I'.

My mom puts life this way. She says, *"We weren't put in this vineyard simply to eat the grapes."*

Baseball helped me understand life – it taught me to think ahead. Hear me out and compare life to a baseball game.

Here's my second love and lessons I learned from – baseball! Could it actually be that we aren't on this 'diamond' just to field pop flies?

Burns Alston

"A kindly neighbor just snow-plowed our walks," I gratefully think to myself. *"Another drove in today's blizzard to help my Mom bring in my lunch. How nice! At least Job, like me, still had some friends who didn't completely desert him! You know, I have friends who have severe pain all day and night. You sure don't have to look far to see someone you wouldn't quickly trade places with,"* I say to myself as I shake my head. *"Yah, I know you'd rather not have your pains. Us too! But, that's life!"*

Strike One...
Sick?

"*Oh boy! Here I go talking to myself again. Oh well, at least I don't have many arguments and if I do I always win!*" I think, pushing my walker carefully down our long, carpeted hallway once again, trying not to mar the door casings too badly as I go. "*My O.T. (occupational therapist) just phoned. It's funny the help out there that I never before appreciated or even knew existed. I'm fortunate to have a caring O.T.*" I think to myself. A friend just dropped by and I so appreciated the visit. He asked how I was and I thought to myself after his visit, "*Self. Last time I checked you were doing all right. Unless my friend can somehow endure this or take it away for me, I'm okay.*" Then I realized that someone did endure for me. His name was Jesus Christ and He was mocked and even innocently died for us all! Mildly reprimanding myself I stopped feeling sorry for myself.

An elderly woman I attend church with recently asked Karen how we are doing. The elderly woman said, "*How are you doing? Are you just fighting the fight?*" She understood. Our church service ended.

"*Nice of her to be asking about the sick,*" I think, as Karen pushes me toward our car. "*It's really the pits not being able to help other people with their challenges,*" I silently complain to myself! "*Wouldn't it be nice to be well again? In this state there's sure not much I can do, or is there? I guess we just do our best and keep on going,*" I think, struggling to get into our car.

"Today's 'good' thing about this sickness is that I sure don't miss the busyness and the hurriedness – the fast pace of life out there!"

Are you sick of being sick?

A mentor of mine recently died from his debilitating diabetes. It was as a high school senior that I first became aware of this dis-ease. A fellow student had to leave an important government exam we were writing and later discovered that juvenile (type 2) diabetes was to be part of her life. Her life changed dramatically that day.

Questions included … How do I give myself insulin shots every day? By what means do I check my insulin levels and what is okay? Will this illness ever go away? Our bodies can malfunction in almost innumerable ways. Get seriously sick and childhood suddenly vanishes.

Whatever your particular struggle might be, <u>going off alone in nature</u>, if you are able, can often help. You may well need some alone time.

Prior to serving a Christian mission in Japan, I spent much reflective time outside and alone strumming my guitar. The morning of our wedding included a run to a local wood alone for some contemplation. When I first found out I had a neurological disease I sought out the solitude of some nearby ranchland.

I visited with a long-time friend today. This person, maybe like someone you know, battled with, and now lives with the threat of cancer.

The hospitals are full of patients sick from any number of illnesses. In fact, there are so many things that can go 'wrong' with our bodies that I'm surprised any of us are even walking around.

It was a well-known actress I admire who, upon facing her own breast cancer, in response to people's, *"Why you?"* replied, *"Why not me?"*

We can be pained in this life any number of ways. You may have ignorantly believed your pain is unique. You may have felt alone, but as the Bible reads, that thought is quite normal. *"...I have no man likeminded who will naturally care for your (my) state. For all seek their own..."* (Philippians 2:20,21, word added).

Many likely know the pains of sickness as it touches us all to some degree. If you don't encounter some pain then you just haven't been looking around.

It's true that many people don't take time to actively show they care, but I have learned that there are many sincere, caring souls, too. Thank heaven we have them!

Our pains and trials come with purpose. Sure, you may feel somewhat abandoned at first, but believe it or not; troubles are an integral part of a loving God's plan. God even says so. *"...for without sufferings they (that's you and me) could not be made perfect"* (Hebrews 11:40, words added).

For many of us illness is a challenge. A challenge, which is screaming, *"Now you especially need to take charge of **your** life! Make whatever course corrections might be needed and keep a going."*

Being healthy makes most people feel invincible, but at some point most get sick. Are you sick? Maybe you're just 'getting ready'.

Are you tired, tired, tired? If so you're bound to get sick unless you change. The fast pace and stress of life can make it difficult, and even seem impossible, to be still and to remain healthy, but as before mentioned, regular times of stillness are essential to our well-being. The very sick know that at least one 'gift' sickness brings them is time.

I know it's early to discuss this, but whatever your challenge, your trust in God (100%) and the realization of your own nothingness are the beginning of your healing.

Perhaps you have felt like no one can understand completely your particular situation, but the writer of Hebrews says Christ has felt what you are now experiencing. *"For we have not a high priest (Christ), which cannot be touched with the feelings of our infirmities; but was in all points tempted (tried) ... Let us therefore come (to Him) boldly...and find grace to help in time of need"* (Hebrews 4:15-16, words added).

A few years ago our family experienced sickness firsthand. So, don't feel too sorry for yourself – you're certainly not alone!

I now often tell my wife that, *'The rules are changing'*. I believe that another component of beginning your healing is accepting that you are sick. Stop all pretending.

I do not wish to sound condescending because your sickness and pain is very real. However, many people wake each morning (if they even sleep) to dreadful pain. You're really sick when the strongest you feel all day is when you first get out of your bed.

It isn't easy to pray everyday and get the answer, *"Not yet!"* Some openly say, *"Prayers and fasting (going without food and drink) don't work."* I couldn't disagree more! I've decided the wise find some ways to 'deal with it' and keep on praying! I never feel better than when I fast and pray.

The Apostle Paul said, *"...we faint not; but though our outward man perish, yet the inward man is renewed day by day. For our light affliction, which is but for a moment, worketh for us a far more exceeding and eternal weight of glory; While we look not on the things which are seen, but at the things which are not seen..."* (2 Corinthians 4:16-18).

No one is saying that your particular suffering is not very difficult. It certainly does not seem like a 'moment' or that your affliction is 'light'. Just the same, this verse of scripture does make me feel it will eventually be all right and most importantly points out the fact that there just may be 'good' things about our pains we haven't yet seen. Keep your chin up!

Laws like gravity govern this world. Unfortunately, one of the laws by which God governs this world is that our bodies age, become diseased, or we simply grow weary.

In school I was taught that, *"For every action there is an opposite and equal reaction."* This is also true on the suffering stage. The 'opposite and equal' here are the things one now sees (in light of their illness), learns, and the character traits enhanced by challenge.

Engraved permanently on my heart is the image of the beautiful, young mother my wife and I once visited. She now lay, in her early twenties, in a bed alone as a brain tumor ravished her young body. She had worked honorably for her God and now her young husband cared for their newborn child - alone.

A fairly young man came in his front door the other day and said to his wife, *"Honey, I think you better get me to a hospital!"* When questioned it was clear that he had experienced a heart attack!

The next morning he was flown to a large city for open-heart surgery. When asking the doctor what his options were, I'm told the surgeon replied, *"Well, you could jump out the window."*

A young lady got into an SUV for a weekend ski trip. She stopped along a snowy highway to help someone who was stuck. Good thing, right? Nevertheless, she was run over by a semi and lives each day with her pain and paralysis. The entire family hurts. Doesn't seem fair does it?

Another, now diseased friend of mine leaned over to me in church once and said, *"I just don't get it! Of all the people to get sick, why you?"* I later thought as the well-known actress did, *"Why not me? Some of the most Christ-like people I know are sick."*

If you suffer in any way, <u>read and believe Hebrews chapter 12.</u> This sure helped me better understand all trials.

Here's just a taste of the Bible's words. *"…Ye have not yet resisted unto blood…despise not thou the chastening of the Lord… For whom the Lord loveth he chasteneth…* (Hebrews 12:4-6).

Why does He love us so much? Right? In the musical "Fiddler on the Roof", Tevya prayed something like, *"Dear God, we know we are the chosen people, but once in a while, couldn't you please choose somebody else to love?"*

One thing I certainly know is that people need to trust God in their illness and not give the final word to any doctor even though many docs do their best. There are doctors of the body. There are doctors of the spirit, but it is Christ himself who is the master physician. It is from this 'doctor' we can gain the most!

MD's are not gods even though many do dress in white! Pay attention to your doctor(s), they are very knowledgeable and possess skills that can often help us, but do not believe everything you're told. You are the one who is most responsible for your own health.

One friend we cherish went to see the doctor and was told she had six months to live. That was over twenty years ago!

Our own son was once scheduled for surgery and hospitalized in a large city's cancer clinic. We did not go ahead because those who cared for him most felt this decision to operate was made too quickly. We just didn't feel right. We picked him up out of his hospital bed. He avoided a serious lymphoma surgery and the unnecessary puncturing of a lung and he was later told he did not need an operation and he most certainly had no cancer!

As his father I had the right to bless him. I did this twice and both times my 'inner' voice said that the doctors would be *"Surprised"*. We witnessed a miracle recovery.

I don't entirely understand, but on one of Canada's premier hikes, the West Coast Trail (alongside the ocean), I previously had witnessed what to me was another manifestation of God's wonderful power. My fellow hiker and the second adult on this hike and I had received, by naval radio, contact that for at least the next few days we were in for a severe storm at sea. Storm-tossed, fellow fleeing hikers were even giving us their precious food supplies to lighten their packs. I suppose they felt it best to leave at once!

The Boy Scouts with us huddled in their wind and rain blown tents – one boy nearly hypothermic. This second leader, recently home from his Christian church mission, suggested we pray and implore God to calm those waters. At midnight we huddled near our small fire (the only fire on that large beach) and marveled as the storm ceased and we watched Venus as she brilliantly reflected off those now still waters.

You don't have to believe this, but it happened! With God, I've decided anything is possible.

I find it very interesting how quickly some accept miracles of the past and how slow some are when it comes to miracles today or in the future.

I once heard an unforgettable line in a church sermon. The speaker quoted Humpty Dumpty where he said, *"All the king's horses and all the king's men couldn't put Humpty together again."* He then asked us a most interesting question. He queried, *"But what about the king?"* Does your God lack power?

It was while teaching grade six that I learned the big question to understand in all of life is, 'Why'?

For example, in math, as soon as students understood the 'why' behind carrying the one when adding (that it was really a ten) it made all the difference. Understanding your suffering, that it has purpose and that you're never totally alone, can help too.

Our lives are full of the challenging. King David cried out, *"Have mercy on me, O Lord; for I am weak…heal me for my bones are vexed…. I am weary with my groaning: all the night make I my bed to swim; I water my couch with my tears"* (Psalms 6:2-6).

Maybe, if even mighty King David had cause to wet his pillow by night, we can endure our own hardships too.

An acquaintance of mine just visited. He has been in the psychiatric ward of the hospital. It was good to see him again and it helped me realize that a whole lot of people suffer in their mind – they have an illness that cannot be seen on the physical exterior. I don't pretend to understand depression, but I have learned one thing about mental illness - it's real! No matter how dark you might be, know this, and I reemphasize, you're never entirely alone with Christ in your life.

Depressed people are often in denial of their own body chemistry and because their brain is not physically well, they need to <u>seek out professional help!</u> You likely did nothing 'wrong'. You may not even want to do those Christian things you feel you're 'supposed to want to do'. This is many people's illness and it's tough!

The truth is, depression is not your fault – it's often inherited and – it might be that this is your lifelong challenge.

I can only imagine your pain and if you suffer the pains of suicide, which often attends mental sickness, my heart goes out to you! Remember, you're not alone!

As mentioned earlier, there are almost innumerable ways you can be ill. Perhaps the least understood are mental disorders.

If you have been given such an illness please accept this disorder and move on as best you can. To all who must face such demons I believe many can cage the 'monsters' and these must be controlled, not ignored. I realize these illnesses are sorely misunderstood.

In my spare time I used to love pruning trees. I was taught that trees have rings in their trunks and that the smallest rings come in times of difficulty - like a season of drought – hardship.

Like a tree we are wise to 'cut back' on things we do when sick or very tired and focus on getting better. If you think you're irreplaceable – you're wrong!

Maybe, just maybe, you need to find a way to make the most of your current situation. I know that it's hard and it still doesn't seem fair.

Why is a dear friend destined to a life in her wheelchair and another who just lost her husband forced to craft a new life with their small child? Remember, easy isn't always better!

The Bible helps us understand and accept this reality a bit better, but the bottom line is – it takes faith (trust) in God!

Our family is currently learning much; maybe more than we otherwise would or could have understood. Our sickness is rare, but certainly not unique, and has prompted us to closely examine what we really believe.

Do we really believe what we say we believe – or does our belief only go so far before we stop? Here are some things I really believe with a few verses from the Bible to 'back me up'.

1. We have always existed. - (Job 38:7) - *We even shouted for joy!*

2. Just being born took much trust and bravery. - (Hebrews 12:8) – *Life isn't meant to be easy. We are not deserted – even if we feel like it.*

3. Life is governed by natural laws – (Genesis 1) – *Think about the rising of the sun. Do you believe the creation (organization)? To me, all things denote that God lives.*

4. All people are God's – His children. - (Hebrews 12:5) - *He says we are His sons and daughters.*

5. The opportunity is given us to become more Christ-like when something is taken away. - (Isaiah 28:9,10) – *We surely don't learn much in our prosperity alone.*

6. There is a purpose to life. - (Ecclesiastes 3) - *We can count on this!*

7. With God, nothing is impossible. - (Romans 4:18-21) - *Hope against hope.*

8. God is loving and merciful. - (Isaiah 55:7) - *He (God) will abundantly pardon.*

9. Unpleasant challenges come to good people. - (Job 1:1) - *Perfect man?*

10. What lasts are loving relationships, knowledge, and memories. - (2 Corinthians 4:18) - *We haven't lost anything, that really lasts!*

11. A wise person does not bargain with God – they covenant. - (Genesis 9:15) - *We can make sincere promises – but no strings attached – thy will be done!*

12. The way to God is narrow and straight. - (Luke 13:24) - *We can't afford too much wandering.*

13. We'll all return home to Christ again one day. - (Hebrews 11:13) - *We trust this will be a great day if we just prepare now.*

There is a very valid reason that the sick are told to 'have the patience of Job'. You may not feel that you deserve this.

Jesus Christ's chief apostle Peter once said, *"…but if, when ye do well, and suffer for it, ye take it patiently, this is acceptable with God"* (Peter 2:20).

Another friend of mine just visited. She told me of three prominent churchmen in her Florida community (good men) who became ill and died 'young'. We should not be surprised.

These closing scenes are natural. Death is a necessary part of life. We don't have one without the other.

It's fall in our part of the world. I went for a tour of autumn leaves. They were breathtaking! My favorite time of year is autumn. In life, it is my opinion that like leaves, we can get more beautiful as we age gracefully (I know there are entire seasons we'd gladly skip), but then we too must fall and return to our mother earth.

Is suffering at work in your life? Are you asking, *"Why?"*

I don't pretend to have all the answers, but I do know that you certainly don't learn much about a child until you take away a toy or insist it's 'bedtime'.

Perhaps the master teacher is teaching us some things and God is watching to see if we willingly learn His toughest lessons.

Maybe, like my church friend, you just don't understand! It is natural to ask, *"Why me?"* People throughout all history have asked this question. Why do 200,000 people die in a tsunami? What of the wars and famines that take so many lives? How about all those little children who die in third world countries and intentionally have their life terminated here in North America? Some people become hopeless about the state of our world, but...

I say God is a giver of good only. This, I know, is hard for people to accept and understand, but God just doesn't think or see like the average Human (Isaiah 55). We would be wise to view our mortality as God views it.

Since your illness, or the sickness of one you love, I would bet that you have prayed more intensely. Keep it up. Even though the heavens often appear sealed, I know a caring God hears every inkling of our hearts. He just may not answer exactly the way we think He should. What kind of trust is it when one quits?

I feel like God answers us in many ways. He may say, *"No"* or *"Yes"* or he may say, *"Later!"* It's waiting that hurts!

The great American preacher Norman Vincent Peale has hurting people use what he calls the 'prayer-imaging formula'. This does help me in my present state. Imagine, and focus on, your desired state – be specific. The mind is very powerful. Who knows but what your desire might be granted as you hope. You surely will not improve if you believe and think otherwise. And, may I add one thought? I do not believe any reason for your hoped for healing can be selfish – self-centered. To all, prayer + belief = divine power!

Too often, in life, 1 feel we demean instead of honor Christ. A man I greatly admire was once being wheeled into surgery. An orderly for some reason began swearing and using Christ's name vainly. Though partially sedated the patient asked this orderly to please refrain from using God's name disrespectfully.

Since being sick, probably many kind, concerned people have asked, *"How are you?"* My answer varies (most don't really know what they are even asking). On a bad day I have been tempted to respond with, *"Well, I still shower myself!"* or *"I no longer need to worry about getting the toilet seat wet."*

Instead I soften the blow and simply answer, *"Well, it could be worse. I could be stupid too"* or my favorite, *"My body has never been worse, but the rest of me has never been better. Thanks!"*

Those who have suffered a lot are like people who can speak several tongues. They now can understand people and situations that they couldn't fully understand or appreciate before.

In my opinion any good, helpful religion must be somewhat rational as well. It must make better sense of life for you.

For example, in scripture we are to ask, seek, and knock, but what does this mean? To me 'ask' means to pray even plead for what you want (even Christ asked), 'seek' is to study earnestly to better know Him, and to me 'knock' means to fast seriously, take a risk, and to even more strictly obey. Then comes the hardest part. After all our best efforts we must completely trust that God knows best. After all, it's God who has the final say. Remember if you want a good laugh tell God **your** plans!

Are you willing to give yourself up to a total acceptance of Christ? If not, He will not heal us until we do – give up your self-centeredness and simply trust. Life is bigger than just you! Christ himself promised, *"He that findeth his life shall lose it: and he that loseth his life for my sake shall find it"* (Matthew 10:39).

So, sick or not, in the long run it really does not matter too much to God. I believe it is our response to illness and other common, mortal difficulties that God cares about the most.

Some beautiful, sunny days you likely just wanted to sleep in, but the game goes on. Hang on and do what you can!

Do you sometimes complain? It is good for you to <u>shed a tear or two</u>. That's okay on occasion then ask God for patience and be sure you 'flush'.

There are nights many people cannot sleep. For those long nights I speak to God a lot. This helps!

I have a concerned daughter who buys me used books as well to help me occupy my time.

In Doctor Peale's autobiography this great preacher and man tells of his father. Apparently, his dad had received a desperate phone call from a local house of ill repute.

A nineteen-year-old girl was dying and wanted her last confession. Norman, then a young boy, accompanied his dad despite the rather questionable surroundings.

The prostitute told the minister, *"I am a very bad girl,"* and this wise man responded something to the effect of, *"No, you are a very good girl! You've just done some very bad things."* It's all in how we view life – especially in challenging times – like sickness.

<u>Laughter</u> can really help sometimes. A delicious sense of humor is hard to beat anytime. How long since your last belly laugh? Think about acquiring a good joke book. Let's not dishonor our souls with too much self-pity.

Sooner or later our day to look in the mirror and see a decrepit old body may be the ultimate challenge for some!

The heart attack victim I spoke of earlier in my reminiscing is now feeling great! I prayed and fasted for his recovery, yet to me, crossing the veil (dying) will most certainly be the ultimate of all adventures! Death is certainly an event we need not fear.

You know, if a severely sick person were to be well again, that person would try their best never to forget or let life's busyness get in their way of real living. A friend tells me that remembering his hospitalization is hard and that occasionally he forgets.

Another cancer-stricken, now in remission, friend says that she is, *"Living on bonus time!"* I believe that we are all on bonus time.

Some sick have been given a second life. The truly wise person, no matter what shape they're in will spend most of their life's currency (time) on relationships and gaining knowledge – both of which last!

C.S. Lewis, in an enlightened moment, said that he didn't doubt God would give His best to us; he simply sometimes wondered how very painful His best might be. He personally lost his bride of just four years to a painful bone cancer, and later, at the age of just sixty-four suffered himself with renal dysfunction.

God promises us, as we trust Him. *"I will say of the Lord, He is my refuge and my fortress: my God: in him will I trust. Surely he will deliver thee from the snare of the fowler, and the noisome pestilence. He shall cover thee with his feathers, and under his wings shalt thou trust: his truth shall be thy shield and buckler. Thou shalt not be afraid for the terror by night: nor for the arrow that flieth by day"* (Psalm 91: 2-5).

You may think, *"I just can't do this anymore."* Believe me when I say, *"Oh, yes you can – and must!"* For many it may still be in the early innings. Anything can happen. Don't give up! You may win in the bottom of the ninth inning. From my reading

I have noticed that Christ often comes in the fourth watch (like His disciples at sea) just when you are about to give up.

I long ago decided, though it's been said many times and many ways (now I sound like Bing Crosby), it doesn't much matter the pitches that come your way. What really matters is how you take (adjust to) those pitches while at the plate.

"So I'm sick. Things could easily be worse," I say to myself. Starting still another day, I often temporarily ask myself, *"Why am I getting out of bed?"* The answer then hits me, *"Because in bed I for sure do little or no good! In bed I'm pretty much dead. I best get showered, that's about all the physical work I can handle these days. Then I'll find some place where I can find solitude and keep still. It only hurts when I move. How pitiful. Thank goodness I still have my mind! Well, sorta. At the best of times my brain wasn't all that good!"*

Are you sick of being sick?

As hard as it is, that may be your life – at least for now! Live it!

Both my mother and I agree that even if we only get one good, useable idea in an entire book, our time has been well-spent. Write at least one practical idea (remember, don't forget the above underlined words) to help endure your illness.

Please, write below what you will do in your future to patiently endure your individual pains.

_____

_____

Strike Two...
Accident?

"*W̶ell, I'm not better this morning*," I say as I struggle to get myself vertical. I then think, optimistically, "*Maybe tomorrow I'll feel better. I can hear the National Anthem coming from the school where I once taught. I miss those people at school. I hope they miss me a little bit too,*" I think as I get about my day. "*It snowed this morning,*" I tell myself, looking out of our log room window.

Something 'good' about this illness suddenly comes to me. "*I now no longer need to clean the snow off my feet. I get to ride most places!*"

Have you been limited or hurt by an 'accident'?

Diogenes of Sinope was an interesting ancient thinker. He believed that for anyone to be complete he or she must live a homeless, vagrant, in tune with nature lifestyle - sounds a lot like Boy Scouts.

I feel that living this type of life is worthwhile, but I don't feel this is the type of life that is necessary to live completely. Your trials will teach you life's most important lessons and you certainly don't have to go looking for them. Diogenes' lifestyle is inviting difficulty into your life and in time there will be enough happening in the ordinary person's life without extending an invitation to 'trouble'.

Whether or not one agrees with Diogenes, part of people's becoming complete seems to involve troubles.

I will never forget a now humorous 'accident' I once witnessed. A good friend was about five minutes away from his wedding reception. A three-tiered wedding cake was delicately placed near the bridal party and things seemed set to go ahead perfectly as planned. Just then, unexpectedly, a young boy ran by the cake, accidentally snagging his suit coat button on the cake's knitted tablecloth creating quite the mess. I thought to myself, *"Accidents do happen!"*

Another good friend of mine lost his son to an unfortunate car accident. As I stood on that black strip of highway waving a 'Slow' sign to passing vehicles, I couldn't help asking myself and God the age-old question, *"Why?"*

I've avoided serious accident thus far in my own life, but I do know that accidents cause many good people much pain. I have only had a broken toe, rib, etc. Minor accidents and for the most part I deserved them.

A vibrant, young 18-year-old girl went snowboarding a while ago. She wasn't really hot-dogging or anything like that yet now spends life confined to a wheelchair.

What of the person left permanently wheelchair bound destined to live pretty much all of their life in near constant pain – emotional and physical? Doesn't seem fair does it? Thank goodness for a caring mother and siblings!

I have concluded that no matter what happens in our life everything will eventually be okay. Our pain is not purposeless! Hard? Yes! But pain forces us to focus more on what really matters – sounds trite, but it's true!

I once climbed mountain peaks and ran marathons – both good activities - and now I can barely put one foot in front of the other – my wheelchair sits downstairs. Again, it doesn't seem fair does it?

"Why? Why does God allow such things to transpire?"

Many vividly recall the day we removed a young friend from the wreckage of his vehicle. Again our hearts cried out, *"Why?"*

Every circumstance of life I believe is for our eventual good. I know it still hurts, but don't ever accept that God doesn't allow such to happen without purpose. Both light and darkness combine to paint life.

Struggle has me most grateful to all who expend effort or risk their own comfort to help other people heal.

When struggle strikes we need to be there as soon as possible and as unsure as we may feel about what we should say, nothing much we could say would help anyway.

The story is told of a young child who lost her playmate to a 'premature' death. This young girl went to visit the grieving mother. When this child's father asked his daughter what she had said, she answered, *"Nothing. I just cried with her."*

It took love and courage for this little girl to pay her <u>visit</u>, but oh how it must have brought some degree of comfort to this mom! When accidents do happen, as they will, let's just be there and cry.

Still another night I remember a young boy being killed as he innocently rode his motorbike from the ditch to the gravel road. Little did he know, but a pickup was at that exact second using the very same stretch of country road – an 'accidental death' followed and no one was 'at fault'.

Three of my former students, now only in their early twenties, lost their young lives on a nearby strip of highway. How unfair this seemed at the time!

My first early morning clergy call was immediately following a young girl's encounter with a fatal road approach. *"Why?"*

Perhaps you've been in the space where you finally thought you saw a light at the end of the dark tunnel, only to be 'hit by a train'. Your father dies, Mom gets old, or a dear friend loses a job. Perhaps you once believed there was actually a limit to your pain – and then the pain got worse?

There are few guarantees in life! Just as things seem to be going quite well – bang!

In 1986 the space shuttle Challenger exploded. I will never forget the image of the plumes of smoke falling to the earth. The first civilian (a teacher named Christa) and others lost their mortal lives that day.

It's easy to see God in a prairie sunset, the majesty of the Rocky Mountains, or from space, but when we can see God at work even in our suffering then I think we are getting close to a real trust in and understanding of God.

The other day I memorized <u>Psalms 23</u>. This psalm comforts anyone at times of sickness or accident. *"The Lord is my shepherd, I shall not want, He maketh me to lie down in green pastures. He leadeth me beside still waters. He restoreth my soul. He leadeth me in the paths of righteousness for His name sake. Yea, though I walk through the valley of the shadow of death, I will fear no evil..."* (Psalms 23).

My family, and I currently face the valley of the shadow of death (as we all do eventually), which this psalm talks about. And do you know what! Death has lost most of it's sting. Knowing this psalm by heart may help you to see how blessed you are and have been – despite your current pain.

Fortunately, I have only fallen down twice. My G.P. says he'll stop by our home and use some 'crazy glue' to patch me up as needed. I have the funny image of him, hair standing on edge, like some nutty Doctor rummaging in his black leather bag for his tube of crazy glue, then finally applying it to my future wounds.

My wife, Karen, and I have off-trailed many places. Beautiful, emerald Rocky Mountain lakes were no accident. The red rock of Mokowanis in Glacier National park was no accident (there's even a hillside toilet you must see to believe). Then there was some bushwhacking to climb Forum Peak late in the season, which almost cost friends and us our lives – no accident either!

We have hiked some of North America's most rugged terrain. Probably the most obstacle-ridden hike was through Alaska's Chilkoot Pass. The old gold rushers used this trail in the late 1800s, but as we personally encountered swamps, boulders, and snow etc. (and yes, it was July) we just stuck it out, stayed to the trail and when the going got really tough (so much fog we could not see) there were orange pipes marking the safe pathway to follow. In life with Christ's help we can even traverse safely the rocky, thorny, uphill pathway of struggle.

Letting faith and trust in Christ guide your life will prepare you for the times in life that your 'trail' might be temporarily shrouded and dimmed.

We all struggle. Accidents happen and often hurt. We need to reach the point where we decide, *"Yes, I will live with God and suffer this pain one day at a time and do whatever it takes, or we accept that this is just too hard."* Until we accept that God is in charge, we will not be at peace.

Many things, which happen to us, with our limited view, will eventually become clear if we're patient and keep faith in God.

Accidents and our illnesses are an integral part of mortality.

While teaching sixth grade we looked forward and did some planning for our ten-year graduation reunion. I wish you could have seen their faces when I said, *"Some of you will not be in attendance due to illness or accidental death."*

Sure enough each reunion thereafter required a moment of silence. I was right and would then point to a wall showing deceased former students and tell their stories.

In baseball I found out that the best team doesn't always win and sometimes while doing your darndest at running the bases the ball hits you – and **you** are out even though you were trying your best. It just didn't seem fair!

"I think today I'll be adventurous and sit out on our deck," I say to myself while nodding my head.

The wind picks up and changing my mind I decide, *"I guess not. I suppose I'll just do some good reading inside. Isn't the tree outside my window beautiful?"* I question to myself as I slink down into my big, comfortable, black chair? *"I sure enjoy the hot, vibrating pad our married kids almost threw away,"* I say out loud. *"Now that would have been my loss!"* I continue to myself, opening a favorite book and settling in.

Have you been limited or hurt by an accident?

If so, this, I believe, was no 'chance' occurrence. There is purpose in your troubles!

Write down at least one consoling idea you will use from the above chapter.

_____

_____

Strike Three...
Money Challenges?

"*I made it!*" I mumble to myself. *"Now, tell me again why I got up?"* I question out loud. Slowly pushing my walker the thought that crosses my mind first and then is quickly erased is, *"This looks like a very long day!"* Picking up the phone and using my clearest voice I pretend I'm normal (I do hate pretending, but I feel I must) and say to our neighbor, *"Hi, how yah doing? (I hope he understood my slurred speech),"* and then a smile comes to my face as I remember two solutions to my illness that were given by former school staff members. One teacher said I just needed to drink a good quality beer. That I may as well feel good if I'm going to walk and talk like a drunk. Also, I became sick just after shaving off my mustache of 20+ years. Another well-meaning staff member suggested it might be the Samson syndrome! Samson lost his strength just after someone cut off his hair. Still giggling I think, *"If I really thought these ideas would work, I might try them! Know what else is a positive by-product of this disease? I look and move like a drunk, but I don't have to buy drinks - ever!"*

Is it wrong to die rich?

Interesting question. Not something most people ever have to worry about, right?

Truth is – many people do die rather wealthy and so this question is worth thinking about.

The Bible teaches that the love of money (not the money itself) is the root of all evil. I agree with this statement, but I would like to add a thought or two of my own. I feel that it is the unequal distribution of wealth that is at the root of our world's concerns.

Truth is often stranger than fiction. A lady friend I greatly admire and an annual visitor stopped by to visit this Christmas season with her husband and related to me the following story. She was doing some seasonal shopping in the United States, when through no fault of her own, she was witness to two men shooting and killing each other. And what was this violent fight over? A toy! Yes, the men were fighting over a toy – something money could buy. We'd all be wise to have money and the things it can buy in the proper place.

The other day I read that people go through three stages in life. First, we acquire. Then, we accumulate. Finally, (if we're wise we do this before we are gone) we give away.

I have seen many hard circumstances caused largely by poverty, but if you ask me, too much ease and prosperity has ruined just as many or more lives recently.

Did you know that in the United States alone there are approximately 1/5th of the people, that's one in every five, who are living in poverty? Imagine the rest of the world!

I dream of a society who cares so much about the poor that there are none. I dream of a society that uses education and other resources to really reach and help the poor. I laugh to myself as I listen to possible future world leaders talk about their supposed concern for the poor, yet they themselves own many houses – some of these are mansions by the standards of an everyday person.

So far you may have helped our globe become a better place to live because of your willingness to lovingly help and share with your fellow beings, but can we do more? Yes, we now need to give and do even more.

As a young child in the 1950s it was my job to door to door deliver a newspaper called the "Star Weekly." Early each Saturday morning I'd set out on my route. I will never forget the home of a 'poor' family that I often got to glimpse. I don't know how many bunk beds can be squeezed into one tiny space, but they did it! This family even still used an old outhouse as their bathroom.

The strange thing to me was that these people seemed so content and so happy.

I often consider a seeker of happiness who is told that if he can find a truly happy man, that man will give him half of his shirt. He finds what he thinks to be a very happy man and in asking for one half of the fellow's shirt he finds this man's happiness to be a phasod. Finally, after much searching a truly happy man is discovered, but guess what? He owned no shirt!

I was never rich in money, but then I never cared much for money or things it could buy. I simply need enough to cover my needs – sufficient. *"There is that maketh himself rich, yet hath nothing: there is that maketh himself poor, yet hath great riches"* (Proverbs 13:7).

I can think of many wonderful commodities that money cannot buy.

Sometimes our well-meaning children suggest we build a new, wheelchair accessible house and I simply tell them that this home (not just a house) is not for sale.

Dad never was rich in money, but he always seemed to be giving his things away - a watch to a local Hutterite (local

Amish-type people), his coat to someone who needed one more than he.

Mom tells me that as a young boy in the dirty thirties when many were jobless, my Grandpa Joe, who was fortunate enough to have a secure job with a local grain elevator company, had Dad deliver by wagon, sacks of freshly ground flour to the poor and needy. I learned at my dad's funeral just how generous he had been to the people around him. Why is it that it takes a separation for us to sometimes really appreciate – even notice the good in another?

I believe we (all people regardless of earthly wealth) are God's children and one day we'll all account to Him – even for how we used or failed to use 'our' money. To me, our God will judge us on criteria of far more worth than money.

You may be one who has a substantial income and as a result, you have excess money. I believe that with having excess money there also comes the duty of sharing, unannounced and uncredited in this life.

In 2 Corinthians 8:14 we read, *"...at this time your abundance may be a supply for their (the poor's) want, that their abundance also may be a supply for your (the wealthy's) want..."*

It sounds to me like we need and can help each other. If you disagree, maybe you should make sure you own money and that money does not own you!

The Bible continues, *"...He which soweth sparingly shall reap also sparingly; ...so let him give not grudgingly, or of necessity: for God loveth a cheerful giver"* (2 Corinthians 9:6-7).

I feel we chose this life and its seeming injustices long ago. Hard to believe, but we chose some hardships – even financial for some of us.

A fellow in a recent L.A. earthquake and fire had his luxurious house burn to the ground. He said something like, *"It's okay. It's only a house. My wife and children are all unharmed. We can build another house."* Now, that's where money belongs!

Alexander Pope, a great English poet, felt that Satan is wiser today and that he tempts many by making people dollar-rich – not poor. Could our prosperity be a struggle too?

Just the other day a local newsman said that one of four Americans (not one in five) live at or below the poverty line – ten thousand and some dollars per year for a single and just twenty thousand and some for a family of four.

In the U.S., the average C.E.O. is said to make more money than this in a single day. To me, this is not right!

If I could change just one thing on our planet it would be the unequal distribution of wealth! Get rid of the 'have's' and the 'have nots'.

In my mind, we have come far, but our world has far to go in becoming a safe, comfortable dwelling for **all** people. I believe we are to reach a place where there is no poor among us – where we even have all things in common. *"And all that (truly) believed were together (on the same page) and had all things common…as every man (woman and child) had need"* (Acts 2:44,45 words added).

How do we get the wealthiest, most educated, and perhaps a bit prideful to really help the poorest, unlearned, yet, humblest of people? How do we get everyone to realize that they benefit each other most when they share?

Certainly there's nothing wrong about having extra money, but in light of recent economic crisis and rising energy costs all people need to be prudent. I wonder if it is not wrong to have died wealthy and not have done the maximum good we could do with the wealth with which we have been blessed while here.

I admire the world's philanthropists. Former U.S. President Bill Clinton appeared on Larry King Live in September 2007. He was promoting his new book entitled "Giving." It is Bill's assumption that we all need to give more of our time, talents, and money if ever this world is to reach a state of equality.

I know and appreciate that a famous talk show host built a school for girls in Africa – I really do! But something also 'rang a bell' when Mother Teresa felt we really give only when it hurts!

The story is told of a wealthy man who publicized his own philanthropy. When he got to the other side he was told he would now live in a disheveled, old hut. When he asked for his mansion and reported all his good deeds and generosity in this life, he was told that he had already received his reward publicly while on earth. *"...Mind not high things. But condescend to men of low estate. Be not wise in your own conceits"* (Romans 12:16).

Christ himself taught that it was really the widow's mite that mattered most. *"And he called unto him his disciples, and saith unto them...this poor widow hath cast more in, than all they which have cast into the treasury: For all they did cast in of their abundance: but she of her want..."* (Mark 12:42,43).

Her giving hurt! Remember the rich young man? He went away sorrowing when asked to give of his wealth to the poor and to follow Christ. How are you doing?

I like what a man recently talking at his own Father's funeral said, *"Dad was never encumbered by too much money in this life!"* This wise, now deceased, friend had always placed people above the accumulation of money!

Dad used to tell the story of Billy Sunday, an old baseball player turned evangelist. Apparently, Billy had just finished a series of talks, to which the local banker refused to attend because to him, Billy was stealing people's money. Shortly thereafter Billy came walking into the bank. A poor widow had given him a $5 cheque, but couldn't really afford it. In fact, the bank would foreclose on her $1500 dollar debt soon. Billy promptly tore up this widow's cheque and asked the gruff, old banker if he'd take his $1500 cheque to pay for this widow's mortgage.

Yes! I'd rather see a sermon than hear one any day.

In Matthew chapter six we read, *"Lay not up for yourself treasures upon earth, where moth and rust doth corrupt...But lay up for yourselves treasures in heaven..."* (Matthew 6: 19,20).

Many of this world's kindest are without much money. The 'rich' and the 'poor' have much good to offer (teach) each other.

It has been wisely stated that the sorry look back, the worried look around, but the faithful (often the poor I've noticed) look after their fellowman (and God).

Some seem to have 'extra' money – others seem to not. Sure, you can say, *"Well, it's their own fault they're poor."* But be careful, I don't think this is always true. Who gave you your abilities and opportunities to earn?

They say about 6% of the world's population controls about 60% of this world's wealth. This is a shame! It just isn't right!

It's pretty hard to make this world better on an empty stomach.

While a young man in Japan, I saw first-hand the size of house many of this world's people live in (if we're fortunate enough to have one) and we in North America want more.

His walk through a store, which seemed to overflow with good, wholesome foods, sickened an uncle of mine. He had just spent several years in Nigeria, Africa.

Put a truly caring, creative person in charge of this world and all people would have more than enough for their needs. We'd certainly spend less on wars!

Like Bill Clinton, I believe in a world that can do better. In a world that really cares for the needy and does not simply pay the poor with their lip service. I see a future world with no poor among people. How can this be done? Seems almost impossible, but I believe that this can be done. We all need to give more!

I must tell you a story. Stopping at a cathedral while away on his job a certain man found himself praying beside a recently deceased man's coffin. The praying fellow arose from his knees and noticed the dead man's condolence book was unsigned. He signed it and left.

Imagine this praying man's surprise when he inherited the deceased's fortune for simply caring enough to sign. The rich must care even more! We all need to stop long enough to think and show that we care too.

All faiths agree on some things. Loving God and your fellowman is non-negotiable in **any** faith as far as I know.

Perhaps the wealthy could help the poor and needy in their immediate community - really give them help! Couldn't we mow that widow's lawn weekly? Give a generous gift with no strings attached? Much of this already exists, but do we give and serve until 'it hurts'?

Perhaps to help the needy we could volunteer more? I know! We think we are all too busy and there is always something to do, but what really matters most? Remember, there are the good, the better, and then there is the best. Where are you when it comes to giving?

I admire one of our friend's who carves out time from his busy life to help inner city youth each month. Way to go!

Perhaps we just do not really care. After all, we say, life's just not fair! Then we go on our way – we just go out for lunch! We need to cry when people suffer and do anything we can to relieve some suffering. This is within everyone's grasp!

The worldly's definition of charity is simply giving a handout, but God-like charity is that we really care – real love!

In many churches people voluntarily donate between 5-15% of their annual increase. This is admirable **preparation**, but if we are to ever really change our world, we must give even more. We must all care even more!

I am reminded of the saying, *"Give a man a fish and feed him for a day; teach him to fish and feed him for a lifetime."*

29

Greed, I believe, is the world's most ugly sin.

Certainly a lack of education is a part of the concern too. Perhaps we can somehow help others learn how to fish?

We all need enough money yet there are many who live, even in North America, with the dread of filling their tank with gasoline. There are many who don't know when their child's next meal will be. These things should not be.

Statistics say some 70% of this world's people are malnourished and unable therefore to work.

Perhaps the world's biggest challenge is bringing about a real meeting of all the wealthy and the poor. The recent passing of a loved one reminded me that we sure can't take it with us!

A truly helpful theology would help us all make at least some sense of this terrible inequality and certainly really good religion must be more about sincerely helping and loving people than any theology.

Having a lot of money is often not bad, but loving money above people often is.

The longer I live the more I realize that the truly rich are those most grateful for their gifts from God and they are willing to share everything.

Could it be that we're all 'richer' than we sometimes acknowledge? The more I read the more I think like Einstein who was disgusted with excess!

My heart goes out to all you 'poor'. But at the same time, one of my American idols (not on the T.V. show) is Abraham Lincoln, who was very poor, but with his Bible and Mom's encouragement he became something. We need to better understand an individual's worth, truly resent poverty, and work hard to make this world a better place for us **all** to live. May we give more!

I never was gifted with a strong arm, or an especially good eye for the baseball, but I always thought we could win - together.

"*I suppose I'll read some,*" I think to myself once again. Then I find myself, more positively, saying, "*Few people ever get the time I get to spend with great minds (in books)!*" Carefully, I move into our great room so as not to fall and scare anyone. "*Who'd have ever thought that Mr. Coordinated would one day be falling? Let's see…what book should I pick up?*" I question, looking over the pile on my footstool. "*I think I'll read about that reporter who was kidnapped and killed in Pakistan. His wife tells the story so well.*"

"Is it wrong to die rich?" Answer for yourself.

Write down at least one practical idea you will employ from this chapter.

_____

_____

Strike Four...
Strained Relationships?

(Sure, everybody knows that three strikes and you're out, but who says so? Believe it or not some people get more than three strikes in this lifetime.**)**

"It's morning again already," I repetitiously think to myself. Talking out loud I say, *"You know, I think my sick friend is right. Mornings are toughest! One thing is true; sleep sure seems to pass quickly! Getting yourself going can be a tough part of the day,"* I continue. *"This morning I noticed for the first time that I'm seeing double now. Our new motto could come in handy – Oh well!"* I repeat this over and over trying to convince myself that this new eyesight is okay. *"We never know exactly what surprise the new day might bring our way. What 'good thing' about this illness could I think of this morning?"* I ask myself. Then it comes to me and I have the thought, *"You know, some people are blind. Other people see one of everything. Me? I get to see two!"*

Are strained relationships part of your life?

Do you have any frayed relationships in your life? Perhaps there is a spouse or a sibling that you would just as soon not discuss. If we're wise life will not be about 'who's right' as much as it needs to be about forgiveness and reconciliation. I know, that's easy for me to say, but it's true!

Philo of Alexandria was best known as the philosopher who commented on and defended the Christian scriptures and Judaism. To Philo what mattered most were relationships. Philo taught that God created man, people could become like God, and the ultimate relationship is a person's relationship with deity.

Unfortunately, many face the pain of strained human and Godly relationships in their lifetime. Maybe you and a loved one don't always see eye to eye. Maybe you struggle trusting God. Perhaps you feel betrayed somehow or feel you have life to face 'alone'.

A married female friend, speaking of her last twenty plus years of marriage told me, *"I've thoroughly enjoyed a year of marital bliss."* When I asked what year that had been, her reply rather surprised me. She responded, *"Oh! I never enjoyed a full year back to back. The days were scattered over the twenty plus years."* We laughed, but that was kind of sad to me and it made me think, *"Our relationships do require work and even then there are few guarantees."*

Strained relationships are of a wide variety and do cause many much pain. Do all you can to repair or salvage what you can of your strained relationships. Nothing is more important! Really talk! Really pray!

An ambulance was called out recently and I overheard the radio. Apparently, a woman had been out all night and was wet and threatening suicide. The ambulance radio called it 'psychotic behavior'.

Sadly, this kind of behavior is often related to some broken relationship.

Half of this world suffers and endures – divorce – the big "D" – the termination of the number one human relationship of life and I know that sometimes divorces cannot be avoided. Divorce may even be knocking at your door as we speak. No one is beyond its devastating grasp. I believe we are wise to make every effort to avoid strained relationships.

Divorce often results in such anger. There are, of course, the adult pains associated with this broken relationship, but there are often children involved as well. I once asked a now twenty-year-old I care about how a parent's divorce had affected her and her siblings. The answer I received was quite graphic. This person responded, *"Every morning when I wake up I feel like someone has dropkicked me in the gut!"*

Children of divorce sometimes drop out of school and other opportunities of life, stop speaking to some individuals, get unsuccessfully married, move away etcetera.

There are one thousand restraining orders issued per day in the U.S. alone! This is an epidemic!

It requires some courage to get married in the fist place, some selflessness during a lifetime together, and much sacrifice to see a marriage through to the end and raise children. I feel one major reason for divorce is abuse – there is great pain caused by this all too common practice.

Whatever the cause there is little, if anything, to rival the pain of divorce and rejection. Everyone (kids too) just hurts – whether we admit it or not!

If you have or are suffering through a divorce and have children, tell your kids one thing over and over again no matter their age, *"It's not your fault!"* To all divorced adults, I love Isaiah 55:6. Memorize this!

I long ago decided that there is really no such thing as pure divorce. What I mean by this is, *"Yes, you might have a paper that says you're divorced, but are you really?"* There is always

Christmas and birthdays to remember and your children are counting on you to remember. There is still the former spouse to somehow assist also. An acquaintance of mine has, in my opinion, done a masterful job at the unpleasantries and obligations of a divorced parent with children.

Though pretty much insulated from divorce myself, there are those I love and care much about who deal with this form of suffering daily.

The words of a regularly visiting friend of mine still echo in my ears! He said, *"I never thought, or set out to have my marriage end in divorce!"* We're certainly seldom in the divorce courts intentionally, but unfortunately, I do think we're sometimes there too soon.

I will not forget the day a grade four student stood sobbing in the school hallways with tears running down her face. For her, Santa Claus had died. She had just heard her parents were divorcing. Sometimes separation must happen, but where possible (it takes all parties) relationships must be mended.

I'm happy to say that this grade four student's parents were able to work through infidelity and save their marriage.

I once heard a good joke about the strained relationship we call divorce. Is it even appropriate to joke at such a time? Certainly there is nothing funny about divorce, but maybe if we don't laugh we'll cry. The joke goes this way and I know those with divorce experience will appreciate this joke. It goes, *"How was copper wire invented?"* Answer: *"Two lawyers fighting over a penny!"* The main winner of divorce will always be the law.

Some will disagree, but... I recall the woman who was trying desperately to forgive her unfaithful spouse. A second formerly divorced woman came to her and said, *"You weak woman! Haven't you left him yet?"* Job's '*friends*' wrongly advised him too.

Of divorce the Lord said, " *For the Lord…hateth putting away (divorce)…*" (Malachi 2:16, word added).

From observation I conclude that most men handle rejection and divorce less effectively than women. Why is that? Maybe it has something to do with male ego? Whatever the reason for divorce, I see no value in anger! It's your future that matters now.

Once I was visiting an elderly couple that had been wed nearly fifty years. As they sat holding hands on their couch they predicted a future generation of discontented children largely because of our inability or unwillingness to repair relationships that may presently be strained.

Some hard feelings or distance may exist in a marriage. Some hard feelings may exist among immediate or extended family too. Some hard feelings may exist between you and your other fellowmen also. Today, do whatever is within your power to make things right. Then trust God!

And what is your relationship with your God like? Be sure to spend some of your time here!

Certainly there are exceptions, but these days, all too often, I believe, we hurry to the divorce courts thinking they have the answer and we often ignore God. Truth is the courts don't much care. It is God who really cares. I know some broken vows of necessity lead to divorce and thank goodness that God is forgiving!

No matter what game I played, especially baseball, I always figured I could win. I'll never forget the day the high school team I coached was playing our archrivals. The score was tied at the bottom of the last inning. Against arguably the toughest pitcher in our league, our runner stole home to win the game. Winning seemed hopeless, but we won!

Some cherished relationships you never expected might have soured. Don't forget that it is wanting relationships to have continued which counts the most!

"I've been reading a Christmas book a sister loaned me. You know, it's not Christmas right now," I tell myself. *"Oh well. Who says that I have to read Christmas books at Christmas only? In this book our doctor author learns valuable lessons of life from two patients – one young boy born with a hole in his heart and the other child struggling with cancer."* As I analyze the book's meaning I just shrug my shoulders and think, *"I'd sure like to alleviate others' pain. The main life lesson our young doctor learned from his experiences that day was that what really matters when it comes to trials is not health, as much as it is the quality of his present relationships."*

Are strained relationships a part of your life?

One answer to most strained relationships is saying, *"Sorry!"* Mean this! Forgive people – forgiving is an act of self-love! Move forward – even if you can hardly 'get out of bed'! It's not easy, but it's worth it and essential!

Write down at least one consoling idea from this chapter.

_____

_____

Strike Five...
Alone?

"Karen has already gone for a run and taken down our Halloween decorations and here I sit. Thank goodness for her!" I think to myself. I recall an ill mentor of mine lamenting over his current inabilities, *"I can't even stir a pot for her."*

"I can relate!" My friend is on a dialysis machine as we speak. Talking out loud to myself again I say, *"Boy, wouldn't it be a gift – a new life – to be well again! Then I cry."* I awkwardly fall into our computer chair and say, *"Well, I guess I'd better check today's email. My list of pluses for this sickness is quickly diminishing, but one plus is that I do have plenty of time! Maybe too much time if that's possible!"*

Are we really taking care of the lonely?

If you ask me the good Lord put us here and it is the good Lord who decides when most of us leave.

There are a number of situations in which we may feel alone and somewhat forsaken.

My dad used to tell me how very alone, small, and helpless he felt in WWII crossing the North Atlantic thirteen times as a young man with waves sometimes engulfing his entire ship.

Not that I never deserved it, but my parents never disciplined me much physically. Emotional discipline? Well, that's another story.

I learned early in life that emotional 'loneliness' was much more effective discipline than any physical punishment.

Did you ever think how alone and lost a blind person in a strange environment must feel? And what about the aloneness felt by a young mother, trying to cope 'alone' in church, with a bunch of her rambunctious children? Maybe we should lend a hand instead of 'raising our eyebrows' and lessen their burdens.

Thousands suffer from loneliness! The lonely may even be you. Sometimes we even feel alone though many other people surround us.

There is something, which seems basically unfair and that is when a parent has to bury their child. This loneliness must be tough!

I vividly remember my grandfather shaking his head, walking down the hospital hallway, shortly after his son-in-law had gone, saying aloud the words, *"He's taken the wrong man!"* I felt a bit of what he must have felt, but do you think God makes mistakes? I don't!

I believe God allows all deaths, but they can still be so hard to accept and they leave an irreplaceable, big hole in many hearts. Just the same, I don't believe any good person leaves mortality until he or she is needed more elsewhere.

In fact, I believe that our physical birth is also a spiritual death and that our physical death is, in many ways, a spiritual awakening.

A short time ago a faithful church member I know had a daughter who became pregnant out of wedlock. Unfortunately, few people visited his home in this difficult time. I think many used the excuse, *"I just didn't know what to say."*

Fortunately, a couple I know visited the home and the father's remarks shook my world quite a bit. The father said something like, *"You know, if we'd have lost our daughter to a death many people would have come by to talk and offer help. We have temporarily had our child suffer a 'spiritual death' and you are the only ones who have come."*

In my memory is the time a certain man was assigned to speak to our congregation. He was a construction worker by trade. In an unfortunate electrocution he had 'lost' his son the day prior to our Sunday sermon. I'm certain now that he must have discussed this situation with family. Fulfilling his duty, he spoke Sunday morning and then hurried home to his loved ones. In my opinion, this man truly understood the gospel Christ taught and lived. He understood that with faith in Christ, we are never fully alone and can cope with all pain – even loneliness.

It has been 20 years since my own father passed on and I still miss him daily – imagine Mom's loneliness!

Oxford professor C. S. Lewis struggled with his kidney failure and a heart attack. He often talked about what he called mankind's, *"struggle for existence."*

There is a verse in Colossians that brings the bereaved some comfort. It reads, *"For though I be absent in the flesh, yet am I with you in the spirit, joying and beholding your order, and the steadfastness of your faith in Christ"* (Colossians 2:5). Paul was speaking to a group of people he loved, but could not physically visit and applying his words to your grief and emptiness can help. The 'spirit' of those who are now deceased are not so very far away.

As mentioned, my mom has been without her spouse by her side for over two decades now. She is most definitely my hero.

A good friend of Mom's, who had also recently said goodbye to her own relatively young husband told Mom, *"You'll survive. You have no other choice!"*

Another good friend of my mom's just lost his wife. Mom tells me that he talks out loud to his spouse often and after sixty years with just one woman I suppose that is to be expected.

Death misunderstood is perhaps the most acute of pains. <u>Romans chapter 4 and chapter 8</u> also helps me. I include just a few verses, which might help you to understand that though your loss is indescribably painful now, in the end, it will be more than fair!

"... he that raised Christ from the dead shall also quicken your mortal bodies by his spirit that dwelleth in you." (11) and *"The Spirit itself beareth witness with our spirit, that we are the children of God. And if children, then heirs; heirs of God, and joint heirs with Christ, if so be that we suffer with him, that we may be also glorified together. For I reckon that the sufferings of this present time are not worthy to be compared with the glory which shall be revealed in us."* (16-18).

Don't lose hope! Our sufferings can have a redemptive quality if we endure well.

I recall sitting in class in 1963 when someone announced over the loud speaker that JFK had been assassinated. This was terribly shocking, even to an Elementary School aged child – *"What about Jackie?"* I thought. How devastated she must have been.

I believe that we need to love and care enough for each other that we actually cry at any passing. Think about your last acquaintance that died. Did you cry?

Most of the world simply closed their eyes when Rwanda's Hutus killed 800,000 Tutsis. We ought to at least cry, don't you think? Sadly, I just don't believe many of us care deeply enough.

More than many pains, throbs the pain of loss and loneliness. The feeling of unfair hurt often accompanies this pain. The widow and the widower need companionship. Nights can be especially long.

My heart also goes out to all you single moms with children. Though you are most definitely not alone (I can just hear the noise), I'm sure you often feel that way.

I recall my time as a new clergyman. A former head of a congregation said to me when I questioned as to what he'd do if he had his time to do over again, *"If I had it to do over again, I'd keep all single moms at home to raise their kids and take away their stress of making money."*

I also have compassion for the childless. Many people want children the usual way, but they can't undergo 'normal' childbirth.

On a cruise we sat at dinners with a wealthy, but yet unfulfilled couple that could have no natural childbirth. They went across the globe searching and when they found a responsive South American orphanage, the children apparently lined up before them, waved their hands and shouted, *"Please, pick me."*

This couple were unable to adopt just one. Fortunately, they could afford financially to hire some help so they adopted several. Way to go! This world is full of many caring, sharing people. Adopting children is a wonderful thing to do. Be persistent!

An acquaintance of mine recently got out of jail. He'd left his wife and children behind for a while. For the first time he experienced real loneliness.

He told me that while in prison he had, for the first time in his life, read the entire Bible. *"For whatsoever things were written aforetime were written for our learning, that we through patience and comfort of the scriptures might have hope"* (Romans 15:4).

My question to him was, *"Are you reading now?"* Unfortunately, he had stopped his study! (I can get away with saying almost anything in my present condition).

While in prison my friend had found comfort and direction from God's word. Why not now?

Life has its trials. And, when suffering yours, though many people may assist, you're really on your own - alone. Or are you? I know Christ can, and will help if we seek Him.

For some, the trial in life is to not yet have found true companionship – married or single.

About half the world is either divorced, unhappily attached, or unwed. While teaching school I saw just a small portion of the pain and emptiness felt by the children of divorce and it hurts as much or more than loneliness. What matters most is that we, each of us, find peace!

If I had a magic wand I'd touch all you singles and unhappily married couples – or would I?

My church is big into family and so I often think about those who feel alone. It can't be easy that's for sure! Just the other day I sat in a church conference, which rightfully touted the importance of family. Near us sat a woman whose husband had just left her and I thought, *"How painful she must feel."*

I believe God takes our difficulties and all our challenges, whatever they may be, into his final accounting. Trust that the 'severity of your sufferings' will be fundamental in your final judgment.

I think we need to do the seemingly 'impossible'! Where fear wins there is certainly no faith – at least not a faith of much help.

If it were up to me, all singles, the widowed, and fatherless would at the very least receive a regular visit. Widows and widowers would have dependable help ongoing for any concerns they might have. Please, don't ask, *"Is there anything we can do?"* Instead, look around!

Shouldn't the homeless have a home and our fatherless have a father figure in their lives? This world's divorcees need real friends who don't treat them like they have somehow failed! All the lonely deserve our hugs, not our judgments.

Religion should make no difference as to how we treat others. We should treat each other kindly – like real brothers and sisters.

Christ's followers once asked, _"When saw we thee a stranger, and took thee in? or naked. And clothed thee? Or when saw we thee sick, or in prison, and came unto thee"_ (Matthew 25:38,39)? His answer was that when you help anyone, it's helping Him too.

Many today simply 'live together' for the kids. I don't know about this practice, but I do know that it is the children of divorce and unhappy marriages that saddens me the most.

Another good friend visits her husband regularly – in jail. Some put her down for this. Karen and I applaud her! And, he better be good to her when released.

Unfortunately, our current world is full of single people for various reasons. Stop to think about it. One day at least half of us will be there too.

Meanwhile, only the ideal world will really remember those alone. In the ideal world we'd pick up those alone and **then** go to our engagements, we'd visit old folk's lodges more, and we'd unconditionally include all.

Who do you know who might be lonely? What will you permanently do to make someone alone feel that they belong?

May I suggest reading the day's news out on the deck with a hot or cold drink each morning or some other alone time for us all and especially the lonely. Quiet time helps heal all wounds. Find yourself a ritual that works for you.

I believe that in life people have choices. Often these choices are between good, better, and best. We're wise when we choose the best – or at least the better and to do this properly takes time thinking - alone.

For example, is it best today to golf with friends or would it be best to spend time helping a significant other or some small child?

To help illustrate how very lonely life can be I think of a young bride I knew growing up. A much older, but lonely storeowner actually purchased her and then had her sent to him from China to curb his aloneness. I can't say that I blame him!

My heart aches when I think of the millions of men and women who gave their all during war. And what about their surviving loved ones? Now, there is loneliness!

Worse yet, what if your loved one was murdered? Many suffer from the pains caused by senseless violence.

Scriptures tell of still other loneliness. This aloneness comes largely of foolish rebellion. Many are those who suffer much grief because of their choices.

Unfortunately, many parents abuse, in many ways, their innocent children. I vividly recall the day as vice principal when I was to examine the physical welts on a young, male elementary aged child.

To all who have either lost a loved one to an ugly divorce, who have never happily wed, or who are somewhat empty because of a death, or abuse - take hope! I believe that somehow it will be all right in the end.

Apparently, according to an old reporter, there is a potentially dangerous rocky outcropping between Staten Island and Manhattan Island. A young man tending the lighthouse during one particular storm fell ill. He reached the hospital with his wife's help, but later died. Though grief stricken and alone, his wife took some comfort from his final words. *"Tend to the light."*

If you are alone, find someone or some meaningful task and do this for now, trusting that a loving God will one day make your aloneness more than right!

If our struggle helps someone with his or her own challenges then God is happy and your effort has certainly not been in vain.

If God has placed some limitation on you, I can promise that He makes all things more than fair to those who valiantly carry on!

We have a suffering savior in Christ! In time, really come to know Christ and His lonely times and you will realize that his life and example truly can comfort you. He was often alone, but then we're never 100% alone!

Perhaps you've been an unbeliever in the past. Know this that sometimes though it may seem like your prayers are unheard (bouncing from the ceiling) God promises that all prayers are heard. We, like spoiled kids, just don't like the timing or the answer sometimes.

One of my favorite movies is "Field of Dreams." In this movie the star, Kevin Costner, plows up his cornfield in order to build a baseball field instead. At one point, when our ballplayers were little, we even had our own backyard mound and corn we pitched baseballs through.

In the movie, Ray Kinsella (Kevin) finally finds an old ballplayer-want-to-be named Moonlight Graham who is now a doctor. A much younger Moonlight gets about 5 minutes of playing time on Ray's new diamond before rushing out of bounds to rescue a young girl choking on her hotdog (what's a ball game without a relish covered hotdog)? Moonlight was not allowed back on the field though at the time he wanted badly to play. A much older and wiser Graham then said one of life's great truths. He said something like, *"Son, if I'd have been a doctor for only five minutes, now that would have been a tragedy."*

This man, instead of baseball, which he loved dearly, had given his life to relieving the suffering of others.

Take one minute if you will. On a good day, would you trade all that your pain has taught you? (I said on a good day)! Would you give up all the love and concern others have shown you? Would you give up the encouragement you've given others to carry on? I do not think so.

A hero of mine once told me that while sick, I might do some of my best teaching yet. He was right!

My Grandmother taught me that whatever is, is best!

We all struggle until we decide, *"Yes, I will live with God and obey him or - it's just too hard."*

Live doing as much good as you can in whatever circumstances you may be in.

I didn't always like what the umpire in baseball said even though they were, most of the time, probably right.

"I think I better take a break. This typing is getting tough," I mutter. *"Now where was that story I've been looking for?"* I wonder aloud. I stumble to my pile of books and realize, *"Oh, there it is! Yah,"* I think, *"one key to loneliness is somehow staying involved."*

As I end this chapter I'll give another plus of this disease. *Another advantage of this illness is that at least I'm only five foot six so I don't have far to fall!"* I chuckle as a good story comes to my mind. *"This one is for all you short one's out there. Apparently, an NFL team was busy unboarding an airplane. Because the news reporter was unable to interview a player, the interviewer chose a rather small-framed, 5 foot 6 inch coach to question. When asked how he felt around so many big men, his answer was, ' I feel just like a dime amongst a whole bunch of nickels'."*

Are we really taking care of the lonely?

Do we really care?

Write down at least one consoling, helpful thought from this chapter.

_____

_____

Strike Six...
Advancing Age?

"It snowed again today!" I say, peering momentarily out the bathroom window. *"I just heard about a kind, elderly friend and relative who passed on. This makes me sad. When I was a young man he took me on a fun trip,"* I fondly reflect. *"He was a fine friend!"* I thought to myself as I shed a tear. As I awoke this morning my EMT wife had her radio call and an ambulance rushed her off to our local Good Samaritans for a 'delta' (that's the most severe) level call. *"We'd all do well,"* I think, *"to realize that one day the radio call may be for us. What day might be my day? None of us is safe!"* I wondered. *"You know, another okay thing about my present state is that at least I don't have to go out in the wind and cold. I sure don't miss those frigid, west winds on the Canadian prairies. The weather report today said -22 Celsius."*

Are you feeling old?

I recall well how old a person seemed to me when he or she turned thirty! Thirty sounds pretty young to me now!

In "Fiddler on the Roof" the playwright's song reminds us that sunrise is followed by sunset, season follows season, and years pass by swiftly. We especially appreciate this truth, as we advance in our age.

Next birthday I turn fifty-five and do you know what? I've realized that by the time you reach fifty-five most of the really important stuff in life has already been done. The children are born and nurtured and for many of us, any help you have to offer the community has been offered. This is not to say there isn't much good the advancing in age can't do.

Life does have its share of ironies. For years I have found it interesting that many rest home occupants want to die – to move on – yet emergency personnel are expected to expend their very best efforts, and often a lot of money, saving these same individuals.

An elderly man is said to have visited his doctor and was fitted with the best of hearing aids. Some time later his doctor saw him and whispered, *"Your family must be very pleased with your new hearing!"* The elderly fellow replied, *"Oh, I haven't told them I hear now. I just listen and I've changed my will several times."*

In a movie I watched recently an older, soon-to-die, man said to an elderly friend of his that you know you are aging when you no longer can trust passing gas around people (I'll let you decide yourself what he means by this. The aged understand) and you never go by a public restroom either without stopping by. Aging does have its challenges!

Advanced age has its drawbacks, but one positive thing it definitely does is simplify and slow down our lives.

Seneca was a Spanish thinker whom three different Roman emperors apparently tried to kill. Seneca's central belief was that happiness was the result of a 'simple life'. The older I get the more I believe he was correct.

My 79-year-old mother visits me almost everyday. She comes laddened with a hot meal made by the kitchen staff at our local old-folks' home.

Another 79-year-old stops by twice weekly to give me a massage and at least temporarily relieve some pain. There are many wonderful, elderly people living in our retirement homes – many of whom I fondly recall from earlier, more carefree, but certainly more hectic days.

A well-known country singer says that he's much too young to feel this damned old. I'll bet you elderly sometimes agree.

My mom is sniffing her eightieth birthday and often says how inside she still feels twenty-one. I'm thinking that many of you feel similarly.

Somehow, I think that's life and I now realize life is short and so I take more time considering what lasts.

We just arrived home having attended our town's annual Remembrance Day service. As a young child I felt that any day off school also was a good day for sleeping in, but this wasn't what my WWII veteran father felt. He took me to the services over the years at which he always proudly wore his war medals on his lapel. There was always a special row for veterans to sit in and be honored that day – due to the advancement of the years I've noticed that this row of chairs is steadily dwindling in number.

Largely from attending Remembrance Day services over the years I have concluded that one day, and it comes to us all, like the kid who draws a line in the sand and dares the opposition to cross, we must each decide for ourselves in this life what circles we 'throw our hats into'. My circles include the names of my grandparents. There was a Burns and Iola and a Joe and Norma and then there was my dad, Cal, and many friends who have already left this life like Roger, Brent, Lee, Barry, Johnny, Joe, Dan, Heinz, Lisa, Ken, Kaye and many others. Do you think these people no longer exist?

I have memories and photos for any doubters to show they were once here – I have many memories of them and though age took some of them away from me for a while, I believe I will see them again. Our Bibles agree! The Bible is another circle I want to be in.

In any Christian's mind to never meet again is irrational! That I should never see them again, makes, in the words of a favorite hymnist, 'reason stare'.

It has been said about aging that it's not for sissies. I agree! My mom says your warranty expires at sixty-five. Some even expire earlier!

Your hands and feet may not warm up like they used to. Arthritis may be your constant battle. Or, maybe you have to endure another surgery for some parts that need removal or replacement. The list is endless.

Whatever your old-age struggle is, thank goodness for those who caringly help the elderly and the struggling! We'd really have it tough without them – our caregivers!

I find that no matter my age, if I am fortunate enough, taking the weekly sacrament (communion) comforts me some as I consider Christ's sufferings at this time. This helps a person of any age to maintain their appreciation for God and helps put our own trials into perspective.

Our bodies do wear out! Sooner or later we will feel the touch of death. This is part of our future – tough as it may sound. We would be wise to give some nurture – even feast – when it comes to Christ's words and example in scripture. Care about your body, but our body simply houses our spirit for a few fleeting years. It is your spirit that requires most nurturing - especially now!

In our Bibles we read, *"But we have this treasure (our spirit) in earthen vessels (our body)…We are troubled on every side, yet not distressed…Persecuted but not forsaken…For all things are for your sake but though our outward man perish, yet the inward man is renewed day by day. For our light affliction, which is but for a moment, worketh for us a far more exceeding and eternal weight of glory"* (2 Corinthians 4:7-9, 15-17, words added).

Often Karen is called out to help others in the middle of the night. Often her calls are for the elderly. How would you feel being one of them? What if you were unable to get out of bed without the help of a machine?

Karen asked one patient, a church going man, while she was on duty as an EMT, how tough old age was. His reply was, *"Well, I'm not the swearing kind of guy, but if I were I'd just say this is damned hard."* Whatever the age and your pain, you are, and always will be, **God's child** – you're never entirely alone unless you choose to be. Remember this! You are God's miracle creation and He is presenting everyone with opportunities to grow – some we would like to miss out on – believe me my family knows!

Inevitably, what we once cared about a great deal (our body – I even once ran three marathons) gets all used up and our inabilities and weaknesses appear. While we still sort of have it - let's be grateful. Let's <u>focus on what still works</u> (yes, it could easily be worse) and somehow, though we may feel a bit aged, let's still care and maybe even share.

Karen, and I used to have a motto for running marathons. It was, *"Make pain your friend, and you'll never be lonely."* So true and especially for many experiencing the frostiness of advanced age.

Scripture often talks about the Lord putting us in a 'refiners fire'. Often the heat is turned up to make us into pure gold. You may be saying, *"Keep me out of the fire then,"* but I believe old age, along with our other struggles, is just that – a refiners fire! Maybe that's why old age is referred to as the 'golden years'!

A knowledgeable friend of ours told me that when a gold or silversmith refines metal, they heat things up until the refiner sees his or her own reflection in the final product. Remember, if you will so allow, you will, through your suffering, become more Christ-like – refined.

The world is a great place, but it can be and often is hard.

We recently met a woman who is now 70 years of age. She has not lost one, but four biological children to childhood death and her family now deals with her own, now debilitating Parkinson's disease. Even so, I believe people can become strongest in their most broken times.

Another woman once, when some care giving workers mildly complained of their daily tasks, asked our daughter (a recreational therapist at a nearby senior's home) a very thought-provoking question. She queried, *"Would you rather be the feeder or the fed?"*

There was no formal college class that day, but I think a most valuable lesson had been taught and learned.

Our eldest son sent me an email called "The Wooden Bowl" just the other day. Apparently, a rather feeble, elderly man had moved in with his daughter, son-in-law, and their 5-year-old. Because the elderly man made many messes at the dinner table along with making some strange sounds and breaking a few glass dishes, he was given a wooden bowl for his food and banished from eating with his family at the dinner table. The little son just looked on. A few days later the son-in-law came across his son in the middle of the floor playing with his wooden blocks. When this dad asked his son what he was trying to build, his son replied, *"I'm trying to figure out how I can make of these blocks wooden bowls you and Mom can eat out of one day!"* Needless to say, Grandpa ate up to the family table henceforth.

In the 'children's' story "The Velveteen Rabbit" there is a place where the Skin Horse is having a discussion with the rabbit. They are talking about Skin Horse and how he wasn't real once upon a time. In this talk, the animals concluded that you don't mind being hugged until it hurts if it makes you 'real'. Old age does this for many!

God has devised a plan. God's nursery is our mortality, and God uses suffering to make us all He can – real!

Maybe you are not a believer and think, *"I have to see to believe."*

Do you believe stars are above you each daytime – you can't see them either, but they're there!

I could never believe something could be made from nothing. To me, this just doesn't stand the test of reason. And as I said before, truth ought to be somewhat reasonable. I have some fine friends. One has dealt with crippling polio since birth. She is a real person. This friend called recently to discuss disabilitizing (is this even a word) our local churches, but it is what she said last that I could not forget. She said, *"Yah, and look at many of our acquaintances, they're busy buying and selling houses for money they can never really keep."* She's so right!

A while back I had just exited the outside doors from a physiotherapy appointment. Much to my surprise I came upon a wandering walker. An elderly lady had fallen. She struggled in vain to right this situation. Helping her back to her walker I thought to myself, *" You know, it's not the falling down, but staying down that really matters."*

When feeling that you're just barely coping, try this. The early monks called them 'breath prayers'. You simply say them along with your breathing anywhere you go and in whatever state you may find yourself. I have three. Be still (exhale), and know (inhale) that I (exhale) am God (inhale). To live(exhale), is Christ (inhale), to die (exhale) is gain (inhale). Also, may it (exhale) please you (inhale), to heal me (exhale), I pray (inhale).

Such prayers may appear strange at first glance, but this method of praying can help one 'pray unceasingly' with no one knowing and bring you a measure of comfort when you most need help. We are counseled to be, *"…continuing instant (always, anytime, and anywhere) in prayer"* (Romans 12:12, words added). This is one way I have discovered to do this.

It's Christmas day. A thoughtful daughter and son-in-law gave us a sign to hang on our wall. The message is, *"When life gets too hard to stand...kneel!"* Wise council.

Years ago our church provided a weekly service at a local long-term care facility. One particular Sunday it was my turn to speak. As part of my talk I read a rather lengthy, often used quotation about trials, which I have since written in my Bible. It says in essence that no pain that we suffer is wasted. It potentially grows qualities like greater humility.

Trials reveal our character – not create it - and it is through sorrow and suffering that we gain the education we came to this earth to acquire. I endorse this belief!

As I read that day in our long-term care facility, one person in the congregation was quoting my very words. And I was at that time young and naïve enough to think that I understood hardship and old age – my ignorance was and is so profound! Some things must be experienced to be fully comprehended.

Aging does have its challenges, but don't ever forget that the passing years have also made you wiser – better in a very real way. And there is still some good you can do. I have long marveled at the positive influence the elderly can be on young people and especially their grandchildren.

Will Rogers, who died 'prematurely' in a plane crash in 1935, said, in essence, that if there are pluses to growing older they include that we generally do become wiser. The elderly now realize that there's not much worth waiting in line to acquire. Grey hairs and wrinkles are hard earned trophies – your 'battle wounds' – be proud to have them and when you think you'd like to be young again, simply recall that school subject you hated the most.

You may be used to independence, but now you must humble yourself. And how do you do this? By accepting the fact that once more you are becoming child-like - God-like. *"...Except you be converted (changed) and become as little children, ye shall not enter into the kingdom of God"* (Matthew 18:3).

Perhaps you were one who helped everyone. Good, but eventually we all must give some of this up and just trust in God – submit your will and carry on doing the best you can with what you've been given and with what you have left.

One of my favorite quotes is, *"Trust in the Lord with all thy heart and lean not unto thine own understanding. In all thy ways acknowledge him, and he shall direct thy paths"* (Proverbs 3:5,6). All of our paths – even advancing age!

Another wonderful thing about elderly people is that they don't say things like, *"It was a beautiful day,"* until sunset, as things might change before the day closes. They realize that though their youth was beautiful in many ways so can be their closing years.

Much depends upon what we choose to focus upon.

Imagine being Christ Himself having the power to end His own suffering. Power to end all pain. I don't know about you, but this would surely tempt me!

Christ must love us deeply to have undergone all He did – betrayal, mocking, being spat upon, beaten, then brutally and innocently nailed to his cross. He did what we too must do – overcome all fears and cares of this world!

It's normal for we humans to want our suffering removed yesterday, but that is not often the case.

I've noticed that God usually comes when we have about had it. Not until the disciple's ship was nearly sunk on the Sea of Galilee did Jesus come. Lazarus was dead four days. And you may, like me, from time to time wonder when Christ will come. Hang on. Christ is coming! Such is his promise (Matthew 24).

Remember Paul's words when he said, *"...For when I am weak, then I am strong..."* (2 Corinthians 12:10).

If the aged don't laugh at their weaknesses, they won't have much to laugh at. Think about buying yourself a joke book. Aging really is tough, but you can still laugh!

An elderly couple had a mutual friend over for supper. The husband was such a gentleman. He opened his wife's doors, thanked her often, and made sure he always called her "*honey.*" When his wife went to the kitchen for something the guest complimented this husband on his mannerly behavior toward his wife. The old man put his hand up to his mouth and whispered to his friend, "*Last year I forgot her name.*"

No matter what our stage in life, <u>gratitude</u> is essential if we are to improve or at the very least, endure well. We ought to just be thankful to a God who has given us time to 'play' in this corner of his 'sandbox' and move on. We may retire from making money, but never retire from helping people!

A famous female talk show host recommends everyone begin each new day by listing several things we are thankful for in that moment. I suggest we all consider subscribing to this practice.

I often consider the 83 year old lady in my aunt's apartment living in a nearby city. Daily she goes around her city streets collecting cans and bottles. She had earned and given to good causes over $83,000 dollars.

A friend of ours has a favorite book. It was written by Dr. Seuss and is called "Have I Ever Told You How Lucky You Are?" On my friend's favorite line, Dr. Seuss says the people he knows have troubles and then he thanks for the places he hasn't been and the people he is not.

It was a well-known Yankee baseball catcher who is credited with expressing the idea that a life is only worthwhile as it affects other lives for the good. Many good, elderly people have touched my life over the years and still do and I am thankful to them.

The best Major League pitcher each year receives the much sought for honor of receiving the Cy Young (a former pitching great) award. It is said that Mr. Young once referred to pitchers of our day, with days to rest prior to pitching again, as 'sissies'. If a pitcher today finds himself in trouble, the pitcher is replaced instead of dealing with and getting himself out of trouble.

In "Field of Dreams", the main actor is told over and over again that even though his trip included much sacrifice he was to, *"Go the distance."*

Often our pains are such that we long for the welcome guest we call death. That's understandable. Even Job wished for this! Try to think of your death as a mere 'transition'. We leave this beautiful, yet pain-filled world for one where no pain will exist. In the meantime may you endure well! I assure you, you're not alone, and one day you will be returning to God who organized and gave you mortality.

Just the other day Mom asked a woman who resides in our local senior's facility how she was. The woman apparently answered, *"I don't know yet."* Think about it!

Today was the funeral service for an extremely kind man. As I said goodbye to many good people at his dinner afterwards, I couldn't help thinking to myself, *"I'll bet this is the last time in mortality that I get to shake hands and hug some of them. Many I care about are getting pretty old."*

An elderly gentleman stayed at our home for a funeral. As his daughters and sons lovingly cared for him I also thought to myself, *"You know, lots of good people wear Depends, but few are so blessed with loving family."*

I loved being the 'home' team in baseball because you get last bat. Right to the end, I'd do my best and I would hope for a win. You too?

"I know that at 55 years of age I'm not fully qualified to talk about the aged, but I do understand a bit of how very difficult it must be," I think to myself. *"Thank heavens Mom brings me meals from the 'old folks home' most every day!"* I involuntarily mumble out loud. *"Hats off to all you aged who keep on trying your best! Your endurance surely does help me!"* as I recall several aged friends of ours. I think again to myself, *"Riding this wheelchair and pushing this walker has to qualify me for something! Maybe it helps when discussing the aged."*

Are you feeling aged?

Carry on!

Write down at least one consoling, useable idea from this chapter.

_____

_____

Strike Seven...
Temporarily Sidelined?

U sing my wheelchair to carry me along I say, *"Let's see. Today I think I'll read! Novel idea since that is pretty much what I do everyday. Thank goodness I can still see.*

I should be grateful for a daughter who keeps me supplied with good, secondhand books," I again say out loud. *"Of course, I'll read the Good Book first,"* I decide. *"Another okay thing about this illness is that since they took away my driver's license and put me on a little red scooter, there are never* **any** *traffic violations (not even parking tickets since we got our disabled placard). There are especially no speeding tickets!"*

Are you out where the rubber meets the road or are you temporarily sidelined?

Most, if not all faiths, expect that parishioners perform certain duties. I think that we all have duties we'd like to perform, but things happen!

Maybe you can't serve, as you'd like to because you've been temporarily sidelined, but is it possible you are taking on an essential duty through just your suffering faithfully?

There are times in life when being 'busy' may not do the most for us! We rush here and there getting a lot done, but too often we miss the essential. We don't properly manage our own time here on earth. Can you relate?

In the orient bamboo is used as scaffolding. I sometimes consider all our busy-ness and programs to simply be the scaffolding as we work to build our lives into impenetrable fortresses of faith. Real trust takes time praying and reading. I'm afraid that our world's scaffolding fatally distracts many of us and often becomes the object of our affection – our life's centerpiece.

If you find yourself temporarily sidelined or centered on the 'wrong' things for any reason this may be your time to really observe and develop a unique perspective on life.

A teaching colleague I came to greatly admire once said, *"Most people today have the five minute mentality."* What he meant by the 'five minute mentality' is that most people sit around watching sitcoms and in the last five minutes all problems are solved. And what did the watcher have to do? Nothing!

Life isn't like that. We often grapple with very real pains – like being sidelined. We must face these challenges and learn to do something constructive about them. No longer will, 'the dog ate my homework' excuse be acceptable.

My only elder brother is now our town administrator. As a teacher, with my social studies class, I used to ask the former town administrator what the best thing was about his job? Every year he would answer, *"The people."* I'd immediately follow this inquiry with, *"What's the worst thing about your job?"* Smiling, he'd answer, *"The people."*

Forget argument, competition, and territorialism if you are presently 'out there'. In this world there's not much worth fighting over - our country, freedom, faith, and family maybe. Certainly, not money, a town issue, our position, or many ideas you may have.

In an office at our school I discovered a great key to success when you aren't sidelined. My 'secret' is that if you love and genuinely care about people, they will respect and love you back.

There was once a wedding reception that I very much wanted to attend. Instead, my wife and daughter went. It was tough staying home alone – being sidelined. Imagine my surprise when the doorbell rang and I found, standing in wedding attire, the young couple I so appreciated. I will never forget their visit, but the reception I would likely have forgotten in time. In a way, I got to be a part of their wedding day despite my not being able to be 'busily engaged'. To me, their visit meant even more! I think I said to this couple standing on our porch something like, *"You both look beautiful, and thanks for your visit, now get on with your honeymoon!"*

You can be sidelined for many reasons. Perhaps you ask, *"Can I stand this? Is God real? What is life all about?"* One of the most common sidelinings is losing your job. Not being involved with meaningful work or presently being on disability can be a great burden in and of itself.

I learned an important lesson about being sidelined on my way to school one day. At that time I walked with a cane. An aid, which worked at the school, asked if she could help me. Of course, at that time I wanted no help. I was being proud! This woman taught me a great, never forgotten lesson there on the sidewalk that day. She said, *"When you allow me to help you, you are doing* **me** *a great service."*

That day I also began to realize that God is using His 'second string' (His sidelined) too. I do not know exactly how God wants to use me, but a great wave of peace and liberation filled me that day. It really is what you focus on that wins.

Perhaps you have partially stepped back on your own - have been offended by someone. This hurts and can also unfortunately lead to our 'benching' ourselves! On the same note, an offence must be taken. Go see them today and make things as right as you can. Life's too short to hold a grudge – no excuses accepted here!

Also, children and others you care deeply about may have ignored or be ignoring your best teachings. Their choices may be keeping them from acting just as **you** wish. This too can cut deeply, but remember, you simply teach not hogtie. We are all agents to ourselves. We each get to choose our own pathway through life - I choose Christ!

I think we always existed and chose to come here now. We volunteered to learn from our pains. Can you believe you volunteered for this?

My wife was reading our local newspaper the other night. It told of all that was happening in our community this December. Then she looked at me and said, *"I sure don't miss all that busy-ness!"*

When a certain man I admire found out he had sidelining cancer he reportedly didn't care too much if he lived or died – he simply wanted a *"jersey"* so he could play.

I believe that when we agreed to come to this earth we also agreed to know hurt, want, and some personal pain. No one escapes these completely. That's how badly I believe we wanted our time here.

Once again, I do find it ironic that people want all that God has (heaven), but say, *"Leave me and mine alone when it comes to pain."*

Many of the greatest men and women ever to have lived endured tremendous personal pain and died young. We revere them – Christ was among these individuals, as were Abraham Lincoln, Martin Luther King, John F. Kennedy and many others.

A great uncle of mine was later in life on his own in a long-term care facility. As his relative and clergyman I regularly visited him. I recall his major complaint. He felt *"stuck"* as his wife had predeceased him. It's no fun being sidelined that's for sure!

Don't ever forget - our personal suffering is not close to our suffering Savior's agony in Gethsemane. Jesus Christ suffered because he loves you. Accepting your suffering pathway, at least temporarily, is essential if we are ever to be at peace in this crazy, mixed-up world.

Christ once even asked His Father, *"If it be possible, let this cup pass from me: nevertheless not as I will, but as thou wilt"* (Matthew 26:39).

Trust God! If Christ himself wished to get out of His pain – His temporary anguish - then it's natural and okay for us to wish now and then that things were different.

Here in mortality, due to outward circumstance, we may not be participating fully, but if we will so allow, we can be intensely engaged somehow – perhaps in learning – learning about God and ourselves. To me a challenge can bring with it an awakening within oneself.

Think of some creative way to reach out. For me, even though I slur many words, the telephone, our local newspaper, and this computer have become cherished friends. Find how you can still <u>reach others</u> and I promise you'll feel some relief.

My scriptures tell me that life is supposed to be hard and some tough stuff happens and must be experienced! Again, please study Hebrews 11 and 12 and learn more about faith.

We may find our full participation limited. Maybe, for example, you are not able to serve your church, or service organization, or work as you once did.

Due to health concerns, a friend of ours was somewhat 'out of order' for a while so her participation was simply to encourage and write some letters. I believe this was as meaningful, if not more, as her full participation once was. There was no permanent 'leak' in her beliefs.

To those who are blessed to be entirely involved I have just one caution. Take time for quiet moments to listen inside and allow God to interrupt and to direct your paths.

Not much happens by sheer chance. Your suffering may seem by chance and seem unbearable some days, but it all has purpose and meaning. God is trying to see how we respond. Will we answer like Him?

At least, be assured, our trials are temporary. Even Dostoevsky, who experienced concentration camp days, said the only one thing he dreaded was, *"Not to be* **worthy** *of my suffering."*

I went into a major store for a passport photo the other day. It was my first entrance in that store in over two years. Know what? I hadn't missed it much!

If you find yourself temporarily sidelined, it also may help to <u>find some meaningful personal projects</u> to keep your mind occupied and focused. I chose writing.

Most of us can still read or write some. "Abou Ben Adhem" is one of the poems my grandma had us memorize in grade school. In this poem, the Lord is writing people's names in a book. When we spend little or no time in life knowing the Lord and serving our fellowman, I wonder if we should rightly expect our names to be listed?

What often appears at first glance to be the closing of a door leads to another door being opened.

Any of our sufferings can bring about depression, but I believe, personally, that with proper help of trained professionals and sincere trust in God, we can beat much negativity and even some depressions. Focus on hope from the teachings of Christ. Flood your mind with His words.

Perhaps you are one who has suffered through a loved one's suicide – or an attempt. I can't help much, but simply say I am so sorry and remember that above all, God is merciful and many suicides are no one's **fault**.

Maybe you're in a position where you feel you can't really help at all. This is seldom so, but yes, it may seem so to you, yet there is some good you can do regardless of most circumstances or pains you find yourself in – you maybe just haven't discovered this yet.

Walking to school each morning was one small joy in my life. I remember an unfriendly man often drove by at the same time I was walking. I simply greeted his scowl with a smile and a wave. I persisted until he smiled and waved too! There is some small good we all can do.

A woman I am a friend with is one of the most generous people I know. One Christmas season she frequented the malls – not to buy things, but to give a five-dollar bill to all she met who smiled.

I wish baseball games had no rainouts, but they do. I also wish suffering was not part of the game of life, but it is. I receive great comfort by reading God's word. You might as well. If sidelined you now most certainly have the time. In scripture I find many who have known more severe suffering than pitiful me. What an honor to be on such a team!

As before stated, in baseball I didn't always agree with the umpire and in living I don't always especially like all the 'calls' either, but one thing I learned in baseball and life is that it does little if any good arguing with the 'ump'.

Today is Halloween. For some strange reason I have been humming to myself the words from 'Delta Dawn' all day. That's strange," I say to myself. The doorbell just rang, *"Who's that?"* I wonder. *"Oh! It's the health nurse and she's come to the door to give me my annual flu shot. How kind!"* I think, as I try to hurry and answer our doorbell. *"Thanks!"* I wave to my former student. *"That wasn't so bad."* I later say to myself after closing the door and waving goodbye.

Are you temporarily sidelined?

Do not lose hope!

Write down at least one useable idea from the above chapter.

_____

_____

Strike Eight...
Female?

*"**S**urprise! I got up quite easily today,"* I say to myself. For some reason, this morning I recall my mom often saying, *"The trouble with teens is they think they're invincible – that drugs, alcohol, and pregnancy will never hurt them. What a joke!"* I mutter as I again reach for the Good book. I ask myself, as I extend my hand, *"I wonder how many church going people have ever even taken time to read and understand the entire Old and New Testaments? Oh yah!"* I remember, *"I said I'd tell you something positive about my ataxia so here is one – it snowed this morning and guess what? I don't have to shovel snow anymore! We're fortunate enough to have good neighbors shovel and if not, snow melts!"*

Are you female?

Mary Wollstonecraft was one of the few female philosophers we have record of. She may have been the first feminist.

Mary saw the mistreatment of Britain's poor and slaves as being immoral. In her book "Vindication of the Rights of Women" Wollstonecraft promulgated the equal treatment of females.

I feel that much of whom we are and much of what we are able to do in life came to us from some other person, often an ancestor, often a female we sometimes never even know. Often we want to 'take credit', but a wise person never forgets those who came before.

Each of us has been given many gifts from ancestors and from God. Did you ever stop to think how it was that a 3-year-old Mozart was able to compose and play the music to "Twinkle, Twinkle Little Star" at such an early age?

Much like talents and inclinations we have inherited, I believe that much of who we are and can accomplish in this life is directly connected to our gender.

Karen is left-handed – she came made this way I believe. She often tells me how she lives in a right-handed world. How true, but not necessarily right!

In my opinion we seem too often to live in a male-dominated world.

As a young boy I was a bit frightened by a particular foreign man in our small town. I often heard stories, how in the 'old country' it had been 'understood' when a husband beat his wife. I could never accept this!

I was especially concerned for this 'man's' wife when told he had beaten her and left her for dead, on the ground, alone in their garden. I have little patience for such a man.

I love women! All kinds! Now, let me qualify what I mean by that!

It is women that make life interesting. Women paint their toes and fingers (be careful! They might even do yours)! Women place colorful, fancy tissue paper inside gift bags. Women make our homes attractive despite the men in the home.

I well recall a wife feeling like her indignant husband had abused her the night before leaving her and the children. Much improvement in inter-gender relationships is still needed.

Lately, I have noticed our sons and son-in-law cleaning the table after we've eaten. This is how it ought to be. A well-known church leader once said something like this. *"The man who can't find his way to the kitchen sink will have trouble finding 'heaven' too."* I agree!

Too often we males are ungrateful. We, myself included, conveniently 'forget' to clean up after eating, forget to open the door, or to change dirty diapers etc. Change!

Often I have thought about the women in Christ's life. A woman was beside His cradle. Others stood at His cross. And still another woman greeted Him **first** at His empty tomb. What was Christ trying to teach men? Women seemed awfully important to Christ!

So, why are women treated unfairly in the workplace and elsewhere around this world?

Only after much protest in North America did women even receive the right to vote in the early twentieth century. Until then voting was not permitted by the insane, criminals, and women – yes women!

As a woman, always remember that without women there would be no men!

I loved the movie about a Greek wedding when the mom says that the man may be the head of the family, but the woman is the neck, which turns the head.

Not long ago, as before stated, woman had to march for universal suffrage in The United States and now who knows, but what in our near future, a President of the United States may be - a woman?

As recent as the 80's, I was asked to start and coach a woman's basketball program. Many staff, even then, felt that girls should not play this game. I almost agreed with them when, as their coach, during one of our early games, we kept scoring in the other team's net. I'm happy to report that today, the girl's teams are alive and well.

We hear all too often of job discrimination on the basis of gender. Just yesterday a news reporter said that in the U.S.A. a woman's average pay is 78 cents compared to $1.00 for males doing the exact same job. Actually, I think, in general women have a more positive affect on the workplace than do many men.

If you have ever played chess you know the most powerful playing piece is the queen!

The truth is we sexes are more alike than different.

I shudder when I think of the abuse of many women in foreign countries who are often beaten, secluded, and even cruelly gang raped or though difficult to believe, are dowsed in fuel and then set on fire. These things ought not to be!

As a former teacher, administrator, and clergyman I was able to attempt helping many and sometimes encountered male favoritism.

It's hard to pray to God in the middle of trials like gender prejudice, but remember Christ's wise advice. *"Bless them that curse you, and pray for them which despitefully use you"* (Luke 6: 28). Tough doctrine, but maybe when in the middle of an injustice, we most need to forgive.

Hope will win over despair and I have great hopes for equality for women in the U.S. and then who knows where this may lead?

There are still many countries in which a woman must cover her face and have her husband's permission before leaving the house. While I do try to understand tradition and cultural differences, the world needs some change. Did you know there are still countries where it is a crime, with severe punishment, for a child to be born out of wedlock? This doesn't sound very God-like to me!

While living in Japan, like a good Canadian boy, I would stand for girls to sit down on crowded trains and subways. You should have seen the dirty looks I received from the local men! I know that they say, *"When in Rome do as the Romans do,"* but we don't always have to agree.

Sometimes others – even children are abused for no good reason – there is no good reason!

71

The Apostle Paul was once beaten and imprisoned just because of his supposed nationality. Paul blasted them when his captors tried to 'brush off' the incident. Paul stood up for himself when he said, *"...They have beaten us openly uncondemned, being Romans, and have cast us into prison..."* (Acts 16:37). May women likewise <u>stand up for themselves</u>! You can vocally do this without aggressing all over someone. Just be assertive! Yes, I know this can be a bit scary!

When I taught 12-year-olds about the country of China I explained that in the name of Chinese tradition, girls are often killed in certain provinces even today so that a parent might have a son to care for them in their old age. Terrible! Sadly, sometimes the traditions of our fathers are incorrect.

You may have been dealt with, or are now, dealing with unfairness because of gender difference. Women of the world – don't put up with this!

Jackie Robinson was the first African American in the big leagues. I hear that in his contract he even signed promising not to get angry when spit upon (today I don't think we'd expect his signature so agreeing). When his mom hugged him after some great achievement of his, people say the hug was as much to protect him as it was to congratulate him.

Jackie did much for black people and was hand picked to cross the colored line in America – I figure it was about time. I will discuss him more next chapter. Many of the greatest players of all time followed his lead. Jackie was inducted into the baseball hall of fame in 1962, so ladies – don't give up!

"It's ten o'clock P.M. Time for my bed," I think to myself. *"I suppose for now my late nights are no more,"* I shrug my shoulders. *"It's getting harder for my eye, legs, and arms to work late at night,"* I think as I brush my teeth. *"Thank goodness for electric tooth*

brushes! *See you tomorrow*," I yell to Karen, our son, and his wife.

Be a proud a female!

Write down at least one helpful idea from this chapter, which you will do. Be specific!

_____

_____

Strike Nine...
Unfairly Picked On?

"*I don't know about that most recent book I just finished reading. It made me sad,*" I say to myself as I pull my body out of bed once more. I had just read "A Mighty Heart" by Mariane Pearl. She lost her journalist husband in Pakistan a few years back and was now 'alone'. "*Violence and prejudice caused his death – too bad – from my vantage point, totally unnecessary,*" I think to myself. "*Why would anyone, even a terrorist, kill largely on the basis of one's heritage? Oh well, I guess that's the world we live in,*" shaking my head and trying not to be too negative. Reaching for my Bible and shaking my head I mumble to myself, "*This world sure is quite the place. Today's good thing is harder to think of, but about my disease a positive is that not many people dare complain to me anymore!*"

Are you picked on?

In the future, let's all choose character over color or any other of our differences for which, unfortunately, we sometimes pick on each other!

I sometimes see that color or differing beliefs has darkened our vision and makes it hard for some of us to see our shared humanness.

In our world, so called Christians have killed Jews, some Sunni hate Shiites, many Northern Irelanders distain Southerners, some Tutsis hate Hutus and the list goes on. For life to ever become even close to fair, we all must not, for **any** reason, feel that we are 'better than' anyone else.

What are you willing to give or do more of to make this world a better place? JFK said it well when he said we must stop thinking about how our country and world can serve us and focus on what we can do in our future to better help the suffering in our neighborhood, country, and in this world.

On the news recently there was a program dedicated to honoring heroes. I was happy to see those honored were ordinary people, like you and me, who had done something to make our world better by somewhat alleviating some suffering.

My parents raised me to accept everyone. They did not believe in prejudice and bigotry in the least!

For example, though we had chosen not to use cigarettes ourselves, that never prevented my dad from inviting over his single friend, the town 'ditch digging' Frank, for dinner – and a cigarette for Frank out on the deck afterwards. This must have been difficult for my dad who was once a smoker himself.

I most certainly have little respect for anyone who for any reason feels they are somehow 'above' another.

In my opinion, the really good person treats the caretaker and the superintendent of schools the same. They are both an integral part of any successful school – especially when the toilet is plugged or a child becomes ill.

I also feel that rather than simply passing through trials, we'd be wise to allow trials (even other people's) to somewhat pass through and sanctify us thus making us more compassionate toward others.

Maybe someday the world will recognize today's inequality and all people's monetary rewards will become commensurate to their hard work – whatever their work may be. Certainly jobs, education, looks, status, color, gender, or differences in beliefs should never be the deciding factor on which we treat each other!

The world doesn't fully get it yet, but *"… there is no respect of persons with God"* (Romans 2: 11).

One of my heroes is Martin Luther King. On my birthday, back in the sixties, he gave the world his "I Have a Dream" speech.

In my mind, civil rights was and is worth working for and if you were able to ask Dr. King he'd say equality is even worth dying for too!

About the issue of equal treatment for all, I think we should never underestimate the power of a prayer. We need to talk – to God and to other people and really get 'it' all out on the table. Abe Lincoln felt that if you disliked or mistreated anyone it was because you had not taken the time to really know the person.

Why can't people just get along? Let's grow up!

I was born in 1954 so I'm one of the many baby boomers. During my birth decade Rosa Parks sat in the front of a bus and the first Afro-American students went to the formerly all white schools. The idea of 'separate but equal' began flying out the window – finally! I was later happy to see video clips with many white people at the Lincoln Memorial in Washington, D.C. It was an exciting time of change and progress.

I also loved the fifties because it was then that enrollment in Little League Baseball in America went sky high.

Why can't all judges, teachers, and employers become blind when it comes to color and other differences? Be fair?

The largest Canadian Indian reservation in our nation is only thirty minutes away so I too have a chance to stand against injustice and stereotyping of people.

No matter what our origin or upbringing we are all human beings. We all bleed red blood, and we all suffer. We're all more alike than different.

A must see movie that I love is "Life Is Beautiful." Believe it or not this movie only comes with subtitles – it is in Italian and at this moment my Italian-speaking sister-in-law is borrowing my copy. The setting is in a German concentration camp during WWII. Possibly the world's worst example of the needless suffering prejudice can cause!

Our differences, like our common suffering, can push us closer or further apart depending on what we choose.

Our sadness, our loneliness, our pain can actually bring us closer to Christ too and to one another if we just understand and accept. We can become more tender – more fit to live with God someday.

It was just 1990 that four white police beat motorist Rodney King. There has been major progress in our putting aside prejudices (we even have a black president in the U.S. white house), but presidential security has never been so high and we do have a way yet to go.

We visited Hong Kong in the seventies. I have forever the image of Vietnamese 'boat people' waiting there in dire need of somewhere, anywhere free where they might go to live.

There was a time when if the world's people had a humanitarian crisis we held hands in our local chapel. Now many of us simply check the newspaper or T.V. and then we forget and have our lunch.

Face this world's unfair treatment assertively and without aggression! After all, when we die, and we must experience death's certain grip, we'll be glad we stuck up for the right.

Isaiah says it well and it is to all people. *"...thou art mine (everyone)...When thou passeth through the water (affliction)... For I am the Lord your God..."* (Isaiah 43:1-3, words added). Affliction includes any bias – any mistreatment for any reason.

As a teacher I studied a lot about bullying. As with all mistreatment I learned that the most helpful thing a person can say when someone hurts you is <u>say to their face,</u>

"That hurt!" And if they respond with a hurtful, *"Good. It was supposed to hurt."* Simply say, *"Well it did,"* and walk away. It takes some practice, but it really works.

A close-up look at death and 'unfair' suffering can actually lead one to God. Our pain certainly proves man's nothingness – man's powerlessness! In fact, I have decided from my scripture study that if I honestly love God then I fear nothing – not even being picked on. One ought to hold their head high. Martin Luther King Jr. once said we should substitute the word courage for caution.

I presently stare death right in the eye and do you know what? Sooner or later we all will die. We certainly don't develop or learn much from ease and prosperity do we?

Most people accept Abraham as a great prophet and man. I once heard someone speak of Abraham's many trials. I recall the speaker saying that the major reason God gave Abraham his challenges was because, Abraham needed to prove something to Abraham. Is suffering to prove something to yourself?

Do you think God knows you – your name? Well, God does! The Bible says so. *"...I know thee by name..."* (Exodus 33: 12). God allowed you to choose to come to this earth to grow and to overcome all fear! God says, *"At destruction and famine thou shalt laugh: neither shalt thou be afraid of the beasts of the earth."* (Job 5:22).

Do you honestly believe we can inherit all that God has (heaven) and not suffer some ourselves? In Philippians 1:29 we read, *"For it has been to you...also to suffer for him."* I am not the only person to come to the realization that there is nothing to fear. As the good book says, *"O death, where is thy sting"* (1 Corinthians 15:55)?

It's just the getting there that is often tough.

I don't care who you are or what difference you may have, the 'bottom line' question that all sufferers face is – Is God real and can we really trust God's promises or not?

Remember, we were willing to experience pain and prejudice (mortality) to become more Christ-like. Through this suffering you can choose to become more fully alive.

Maybe belonging to a majority isn't always the best – though it might be the easiest!

No longer will I believe that trials, like prejudice or stereotyping, build character – instead, as before mentioned, unfairness reveals one's true character.

It is very ridiculous to me to judge someone's character by the color of his or her skin, or their nationality, or their faith, but the truth is, too many of us do. In Acts 9, the Apostle Peter has a vision. He is to partake of **all** food – contrary to his strict Jewish upbringing. Nevertheless, he obeys and in the 34th verse he repeats that, *"Of a truth I perceive that God is no respecter of persons."*

Branch Rickey (white) helped break the color barrier in the game by bringing up Jackie Robinson. Because of his religiosity some fondly referred to Jackie as *"Mahatma."* Many people applaud Jackie's courage, as do I, but I think the other heroes of this story are that of Branch Rickey and the Brooklyn Dodger teammates of the day.

During Jackie's career he was wisely counseled to read and re-read his New Testament and to take upon himself the Christ-like persona – sadly, not the advice many would give him today. He did take upon himself a good, Christian persona and whenever the ugly face of prejudice raised its head, he would 'turn the other cheek'.

Though most people don't know, Branch Rickey is also rather well known for bringing the first Hispanic superstar, Roberto Clemente, to the big leagues too.

One reason that I think I love baseball so much is that it has rules you can rely on and superfluous differences certainly don't matter – it's your performance that counts!

I don't know what it is about man's natural self, but it seems that even from childhood someone has to feel superior and someone must have 'fleas'.

I believe that God's rules fit everyone, everywhere, all of the time and in every situation! No 'picking on' with Him!

I loved the fifties and see that a lot of progress in the treatment of our fellowman has been made, but let's keep improving this game we call life.

"I best remember to turn my clocks back an hour," I think to myself. *"Tomorrow it's back off daylight savings. That bed is sure going to feel nice tonight! And I can even stay an extra hour!"* I smile. Reflecting back on our recent church services, I say to myself, *"Many of our congregation cried today. They feel pained. Oh that I could somehow take away some pain. That's what's hardest about being 'benched'. Not being able to really be a part of others' lives is the pits!"* Switching topics, *"I have always rooted for the Yankees when it comes to baseball,"* I say to myself. *"But, now I also have some good reasons to like the Dodgers baseball team too!"*

Are you unfairly picked on?

Write down at least one consoling idea from this chapter.

_____

_____

Strike Ten...
Abused?

"I remember once as a clergy talking with a lady who had been abused as a child. She sure was shocked when I suggested she go see her abuser and show him compassion," I fondly reflect. *"I wonder how she's doing?"* I question as I tug at my P.J.s. Thinking back to the nineties, *"Remember the person who was counseled to keep a 'Goodbye Journal' of abilities lost. I can see some value of closure in such a journal, but I choose another format and try to find the positives. Believe me the losses are there too, but we won't focus on those! The all right thing I'll share about my disease today is that the grandkids like my walker and 'new chairs' - my 'new toys' to them. Oh that we could all view life as a little child."*

Have you been unjustly abused?

I think that pretty well everyone has heard of Marcus Aurelius. He was a Roman emperor for about 20 years, wrote "Meditations", but is most often known as one of the men who married Cleopatra.

They say that Marcus was concerned about treatment of the poor, slaves, and prisoners of his day. Interestingly, this compassion had its limits when it came to the early Christians who were allowed to suffer inhumane abuse during his rule as emperor.

I believe that whatever comes into a person's life comes from God and is therefore good. I feel that people must learn to be content despite abuse or any other seeming injustice life throws their way.

As before stated, I believe God is a giver of good gifts only, but it's sure hard to understand sometimes!

Like many of you, our family has been touched by divorce. I have often wondered if a spouse having an affair isn't a form of abuse in God's eyes.

There are many people and things that would have you feel less than a full, worthwhile human being – abuse, in its many forms, is one of the offenders.

While living in Tokyo I learned a very true idiom. The Japanese would often say to me, a Christian missionary at the time, *"Kurushi toki no Kami danomi,"* which interpreted means that in times of need people turn to God.

To all abused I say, *"Man's difficulty just might be God's opportunity."* I know. You're maybe saying about now, *"That's easy for him to say!"* Though it's hard for me to understand, I am trying to comprehend undeserved abuse.

I have simply decided that some of the most wonderful gifts come in the most ugly wrapping.

When 'prospering' people tend to act ungrateful, King David said, *"They cry unto the Lord in their trouble, and he bringeth them out of their distresses. He maketh the storm a calm, so that the waves thereof are still…so he bringeth them unto their desired haven"* (Psalm 107:28-30).

I just read a national bestseller entitled "An Unquiet Mind". My heart aches for families who battle mind and moods. Afflicted people are wise to seek help! Doctors of medicine and the mind can both help, but nothing can replace people's patience, love, and efforts to understand.

Sadly, if uncontrolled, depressions may harmfully affect others too and lead to a form of abuse – especially to those you love the most. Depression in its many forms often leads to the ugly monster we call – abuse!

Physical and emotional abuse just should not be, yet, though often we don't like to admit it, abuse is all around us!

I know someone that refuses to forgive unwarranted abuse. To this person and all I say, *"Let the prisoner free! And, realize that you are the real prisoner!"* Paul to his Roman friends said of God, *"...Vengeance is mine; I will repay, saith the Lord"* (Romans 12:19).

Your abuse is not an excuse to further pain. Really accept Christ and forgive your offender if you are ever to get somewhat over your undeserved pains. We certainly can't change someone else's mistakes by holding a grudge ourselves!

God gave us choice and sadly some abuse this God-given agency. The scriptures are clear on abuse and 'unwise fathers' 'mothers' and 'others' will pay dearly. The Lord is very clear about what he thinks about abusers. *"But whoso shall offend one of these little ones...it is better for him that a stone were hanged about his neck, and that he were drowned in the depth of the sea"* (Matthew 18:6). Hard to use tougher language than that!

Lack of forgiving will drive a wedge between you and God. Never forget that if you are not as close to God as you once were (even if you suffer abuse), there is no doubt about who has chosen to drift – you!

My favorite church song is about us all being a child of God. This is the one song my entire family can sing in Japanese.

Since becoming somewhat aware of abuses that exist, even within families, I have often wondered how the abused family member might feel when we sing, *"...hath given me an earthly home, with parents kind and dear."*

No matter what your past or present circumstances may have been or are today, we must take quiet time and obey our inner voice. Stay in touch and don your 'spiritual' armor each morning.

I can't help but often think how one of the most 'successful' female Americans owes some of her success to former slaves, brought here and abused.

I sometimes wonder if uncalled for abuse and abortion isn't what Matthew meant in his 24th chapter, which is loved by all true Christians, wherein Matthew speaks of a day when, " ...*the love of many shall wax cold*" (Matthew 24:12).

We would all do well to remember that life is not a one-act play – it's at least three acts – a before, a now, and a yet to come!

I once heard life compared to luggage at an airport. We fill our lives with many different things - please don't forget to pack the essentials (Christ). Unlike luggage that passes through an airport, we are all headed to the same 'baggage claim'. We were made of dirt and to dirt we must return.

Life-struggles are tough, but they can teach us what we ought to focus our life on and what people really care!

A loving God gave us this one chance at life. God gave us weakness (mortality) that our weakness (abuse included) could become strengths. There are those who wallow in their unjust abuse. Others have made them strengths! It is our job to come unto him. I just say, *"Here I am. Do with me what you will and I'll still be true!"*

I will not pretend to completely understand how Christ does it, but I do believe our pain is for our good eventually and that both my wife and I will see Christ one day when this is all over. This is actually quite a good deal. When you really stop to think about it. We endure our pains well; our trials will make us more Christ-like, and eventually take us into God's bosom. I know you still have to pass through a lot!

Life often seems totally unfair. No one deserves to have been abused in any way. We certainly aren't guaranteed we'll have no suffering here. In fact, it's just the opposite – it's suffering that **is** guaranteed!

My friend, who leaned over to me at church many years ago, believed falsely that living like Jesus taught would insulate one from struggles. The truth is that longsuffering is a quality the Bible says is desirable to possess. It still hurts I know!

Your being tried is hard and painful. What Christ alone could do for you, he endured on a cross and in Gethsemane. Hang on to hope, trust him, and one day he will right all seeming injustices.

No, the affects of abuse may never fully fade, but scripture, sincere prayer, good friends and family, and <u>never forgetting that you are God's miracle creation</u> can add a measure of comfort! *"The Lord is good to all: and his tender mercies are over all his works"* (Psalm 145: 9).

God especially bless you, the innocently abused. Don't go blaming yourself and feeling somehow – guilty!

Let's ponder for a minute the abuse Christ suffered. Yes, he was abused! Long ago, an entirely innocent man was falsely accused, endured numerous mockings and several false trials, was spit upon by his own people, beaten at Pilate's decree, deserted by 'friends' and then, though still proclaimed innocent and to add further degradation, a murderer was released in his place and Christ was made to haul His own cross to Golgotha. He then was viciously nailed to the very cross he had carried, where he hung until 'dead'. Now, that's abuse!

I am most grateful for Him. He suffered more than I can imagine and he 'took it' for us all. May His pains especially bring you, the abused, a large measure of comfort! It's probably hard to imagine, but things could be even worse!

I find that a positive attitude and a visualization of getting well, not being abused etc., makes some difference! You only defeat a negative thought, action, or state with a positive one.

Wise people in all ages agree that as we think, so are we, or so we may become. Wellness starts in the mind. Especially when we suffer we need to <u>find the place of calm</u> we seek and it is my belief that this can be done by coming unto Christ! He can change us! Then we have a chance of improving our world.

I have never been asked who the greatest person I have met is, but if asked I would answer, Mom. I was one of the fortunate – the unabused. I don't fully know why I was thus blessed, but...

There is a certain liberating emotion associated with facing a trial – even our eventual 'death'. We finally realize we are not in charge. We are wise to finally surrender all of our will to God's will. Does this mean that anyone wants to die and leave loved one's here temporarily? No, but did you ever stop to think that maybe there are loved ones somewhere else who are waiting for our arrival.

Do I enjoy challenges, which face us now? Certainly not always! Yet somehow it is by facing difficulty that we become truly free!

Remember, no one ever deserves abuse! Do not let abuse or anyone else own you!

In baseball games I remember often getting a 'bad hop' when fielding a grounder, but that is part of the game.

"Boy," I think to myself. *"I'm sure thankful I was not abused ! I suppose that whatever our challenges, we really would keep our own. Abuse you didn't deserve would be a tough one for me. Sometimes, I think I'd trade and then...on second thought,"* I realize, *"maybe not!"*

Have you been unjustly abused?

Abuse is never deserved!

Write down at least one helpful idea from this chapter.

_____

_____

Strike Eleven...
Lack freedom?

"*Today's news has tornadoes tearing through the southern states killing and maiming along their paths,*" I shrug my shoulders and to myself I think, "*Sure, Alberta, Canada has lots of cold and snow this time of year, but at least we don't often confront tornadoes!*" My mom was here as usual at noon with my meal and she told me a good, true story. Mom said, "*When just a young child, in 1942, our town had a devastating hail storm. It was on our town celebration day in July so our family all drove out to Dad's (my grandpa's) leveled crops, scooped up the hail, and made ice cream!*"

"*Way to go!*" I cheered inside. "*Maybe this difficult time was to somewhat prepare mom's family for the sudden, unexpected death of a brother and son – Ron!*"

Now let me try to think about what's okay about this illness today. Suddenly, I've got it and the light goes on, "*If I weren't sick, I'd probably never have understood and seen what I now see!*"

Do you lack liberty for some reason?

We can be a 'slave' in many ways. There are slaves to tobacco, alcohol, other drugs (both legal and illegal), pornography, chocolate, food etc. If you are currently a slave to anything or the friend of a slave this chapter is especially for you.

I will never forget a lesson I came to fully understand while in the Orient. I was at the time helping a man battling his tobacco addiction. Until that day I had mistakenly felt as though God's rules were a bit stifling. Ever felt this way?

The man I was teaching said something like, *"I could never be a Christian. Christians can't party! Christians don't have any fun!"* Half believing him, I will never forget when, my teaching partner put a cigarette in his own lips and struck a match. I was a bit startled by his actions, but it was his words that left a lasting impression. Handing the cigarette to the man he said, *"I can light this cigarette and smoke it whenever I want. Let's see you quit!"* Who had unintentionally given up some of their freedom?

When the Ten Commandments were given they were not simply opinions or suggestions. They were commandments! They were actually given to keep us free. *"…and the truth shall make you free"* (John 8:32).

There are people who involuntarily become slaves to addictions and thus abuse law and even family. Sad!

Personally, I have never done battle with an addiction, but I know that to many people addiction is a real trial.

My mother-in-law has a favorite saying. It is, *"Too much of a good thing is a bad thing."* True!

Today, I fear that many are slaves to a computer in one way or another. If you spend hours of your leisure time each day attached to your computer or TV are you addicted? Pornography is an ugly addiction, which entraps many in the 21st century – good Christian people, too. I cannot forget two young boys who came to me as their clergyman and had naively found themselves caught in the pornographic web. I think the Internet being nicknamed the web (spider web) is appropriate despite benefits of proper Internet usage. Video games in excess also ensnare many.

To anyone struggling with any loss of personal freedom because you care for someone who is addicted, or are personally addicted to something, please <u>seek professional and personal help!</u>

You first must accept that you have this challenge and admit the problem. This is your beginning. <u>Admission</u> can be very humbling and somewhat embarrassing too – oh well.

Whatever your addiction, admit it and get help! Most of us need at least one <u>'cheerleader' and mentor</u>. The more the better! An addiction usually can't be successfully tackled without such 'outside' help.

Many people today sneak into unoccupied homes, raid medicine cabinets of legalized painkillers, then numb themselves. Or maybe we abuse ourselves on our own medications or somehow support illicit drugs.

I know my analogy is a bit lame, but I used to love last bat in baseball. However, if our team had scored more runs than our opponent the last opportunity to bat had to be given up. That hurt, but it's not even in the same 'ballpark' as an addiction!

"Our one son just visited," I stop writing momentarily to visit. *"Though our pains might be hard to swallow, people in our life should always matter most. It was sure nice to see our son drop by. What a shame when an addiction pushes people we love away!"* To myself I smile and think of my dear friend, who was once the 'town drunk' and who, with the help of AA and a forgiving family, overcame his addiction with all of its ugliness and heartache.

Are you held hostage by anything?

Free yourself. You can do it, but not alone!

Write down at least one helpful, useable idea from this chapter.

_____

_____

Strike Twelve...
Caregiver?

"*Tonight we actually ventured out in the cold,*" I pat myself on the back. "*I'm lucky that Karen will push me places,*" I'm thinking. "*A friend of ours held a financial seminar and so we went. It was nice to see people, but a bit frustrating too in that it's getting harder to talk and be a part of someone else's life,*" I mumble to myself. "*Usually on cold, snowy days and nights I just hibernate at home. If Karen does have to leave someone often comes to 'baby sit' me.*

Now what was good about our sickness? Oh yah! I just realized that when we go anywhere I never have to worry about a seat. I bring my own chair and it's often the most comfortable seat in the house!"

Have you become someone's caregiver?

One of, if not the last great thinker of Roman times, is thought to have been a man named Plotinus.

This man thought that people could only make sense of life through deep contemplation.

Many of you are at a place in life where you definitely need to do some soul-searching and pondering. Caregivers are definitely included.

Most people believe in an afterlife and many, if pinned down, believe in a pre-earth life as well. My caregiving wife and I were saying our farewells to a wheelchair bound church member and his caregiving wife. His wife was talking about life's difficulties when I said to her that before coming into this life, she and my caregiver had forgotten to read the fine print.

At very least I can say thanks to all people forced somewhat into the role of care giving. To paid and unpaid help I ask, *"Where would we people be without you?"* I think we'd be in some deep stuff. I know I would!

These care giving individuals suffer too, but differently. These people must watch someone they love decline, meet their needs, and that can't be easy!

It has been my privilege to have known some caregivers over the years. My own wife has become one and somehow, *"Thank you"* is just not enough. Know that your care receiver is in your debt and is most appreciative.

Yes, it is hard for the sick etc., but it's also tough to be a kind caregiver.

As previously stated, our one daughter is presently doing her practicum in recreational therapy. She's at a senior's home and tells us almost daily how very many people need her and what an honor this is to be one of their caregivers.

I well recall the day a colleague of mine left a much-loved job to act as a caregiver to a spouse. We talked in the school hallway about the early retirement. I told this teacher that they would be greatly missed. The response was that *"Leaving will be like taking a hand out of a bucket of water."*

I told this highly effective teacher that this may be so, but that, *"No one removes their hand quite the same as you do!"*

Imagine our student-daughter's surprise at realizing that two of her current 'old folk's' home clients are my teenage friends – in their early fifties. One friend actually made the effort to telephone me to say how much he enjoyed our daughter.

I'm sure that care giving can be extremely hard, but unfortunately, a former wife had divorced one of my two friends residing in this home. *"Care giving was just too demanding."* Or so she felt.

A verse in Hebrews comes to mind. *"Choosing rather to suffer afflictions…than to enjoy… pleasures…for a day"* (Hebrews 11:25).

When God turns up the heat, remember that he still loves you. Remember the Bible's Job? Few of us are that bad off!

I feel all caregivers need to somehow plan and <u>take regular breaks without guilt!</u> I know you're thinking, *"I can't."* That's natural, but I think you can and must! You have one of, if not the, toughest of jobs. Thank you so very much!

I also believe that the wise caregiver will find a <u>hobby</u> to help them in their times of loneliness and struggle.

Sometimes, I have learned, a 'peripheral' caregiver is unintentionally left out. Our daughter recently came up to me and said, *"Dad, I sure love you. I'm sorry that you're sick."* I knew before, but it was then I really realized that a trial deeply affects many more than just the one person and his/ her main caregiver.

If you have the task of caregiver, please know how grateful your care receiver is! Thank you so very much for all you are called upon to do!

Mom always said, *"There, but for the grace of God, go I."* She was right!

In all my games of baseball, there were many 'others' (like umpires, managers, and coaches) who made playing the game even possible. Thanks!

"*It has to be hard to watch a loved one decline in their abilities,*" I think to myself. "*What can I do for my caregiver?*" I say aloud. "*My ignorance and ingratitude are so profound,*" I further say to myself. "*I'll just try harder to get 'out there'* , I decide. *Yes! Another epiphany (I like that word) I had as we went out among people was that, through no fault of theirs, most people don't even know how sick I am or understand the burden of being a caregiver. I don't think we truly get it until something similar happens to us! Oh well!*"

Thank you, caregivers!

Have you gone away lately? Go!

Now, take time to write down at least one helpful idea from this chapter.

_____

_____

Strike Thirteen...
Oops?

I sit down at our computer and start pecking at the keys again. *"I sure type slowly these days,"* I think to myself. I was once told, *"Typing class won't do you any good! Boy, they were sure wrong!"* I think again to myself. I smile, and my mind races ahead. *"As before mentioned, one of my mentors and friends just left this world. I hope he was brave,"* I say to myself as I begin still another long day. *"My wife, Karen, says she'll take me to my friend's farewell service today,"* I gratefully think. *"Sometimes just being there is the best thing we can do. That's something at least. So, you're expecting another positive, aye? Well, how about this...I've discovered a new sport! There are literally millions 'playing' it. It's called 'Furniture and Wall Surfing' and guess what? The tide is up!"*

Have you made a mistake?

It may have been Socrates' student, Plato, who first said that, *"The unexamined life is not worth living."* It's interesting how most people of the 'religious world' observe at least one regular practice to examine their life – a weekly sacrament.

No philosopher had more impact on today's world than has Plato.

Plato taught that this life is mainly illusory – not real. He felt that the only real things in life last – they must be forever.

His best-known book is "The Republic" in which he describes what, to him, is the perfect, utopian society and the way to best navigate while in this world. I believe that in a 'perfect' world mankind would not make mistakes. The problem is that we don't live in a perfect world. Are you presently focused on things that last?

Maybe you are like me and have done a few things wrong in life. <u>Don't fear</u>! Almost all errors can be righted.

Another ancient philosopher I admire is Aristotle. He said that human life had a purpose and that sadly much of life is simply engaging in 'bodily lusts' and there would be painful consequences if this was all that a human being did while here. He taught that true happiness could only be found in what he called a 'virtuous life'.

Certainly I was never a mean person and any pain I have caused was out of ignorance or momentary stupidity rather than out of maliciousness. I long ago decided that a merciful God does not care as much about the wrongs I have committed as He does about what I have done about those things – changed.

It is most certainly not my place to act as judge and jury for another. However, I do know there is a right, and there is a wrong. So, I do feel justified in judging people's actions and choices.

The good news is that if we've 'spilled the milk' and created a mess (oops), we can be forgiven upon deeply and sincerely changing our course, <u>sincerely apologizing</u>, and then not making the same error again. All of us! Once again, I repeat, of Christ, *"...there is no respect of persons with God"* (Romans 2:11).

As I said, I do not judge others, but I do think all people sometimes are wise to change their actions – improve! It's the best we can do sometimes. I don't want anyone to be fear-full, but the Bible clearly states, *"... unto them that are contentious, and do not obey the truth, but (continue to) obey unrighteousness, indignation and wrath (is coming)"* (Romans 2:8, words added).

Never have I believed that drinking alcohol or smoking cigarettes or cigars was in itself a horrible thing. In my opinion, those who stand by and judge are the ones most in need of change. It is mostly what attends these rituals that is potentially harmful. Of course, being a bit of a health freak, there is one's health to consider as well!

Vivid in my mind are two beautiful, young women who wanted to go to the bar, *"Just to dance."* These girls felt that because they were, *"Listening to their inner selves,"* entering the bar really didn't matter. Trouble is that there were others present who had given up much of their agency to excessive drinking.

Shortly after the girls had begun dancing, a fellow began to stalk them. An acquaintance of these girls fortunately stepped in. A fight ensued and the police were soon summoned. So much for these two girls and their, *"We're just dancing."*

I just found out that someone I care very much about has cheated and broken the hearts of many. Sad! I think about the country song that asks what you will do when the new wears off and the old shines through – then what? It does pay to think ahead. Sometimes way ahead!

The 'glad tidings' or good news in the Bible is that we humans can change our paths and change directions in almost anything we have or have not chosen.

As previously mentioned, I will never forget the pain I witnessed one morning in the hallway at school. It looked then as though one little fourth grader's parents seemed destined to 'split'. I could almost feel her tears.

Still another individual spent thousands on illicit phone calls. With money, power, and sex we can do the greatest good or cause much, much misery.

If you presently are attempting to get 'back on track' please use quiet and <u>time alone in nature</u>. These have always helped me get in touch with the 'goodness (Godliness) within'.

One of my favorite stories in the Bible is about the misuse of sex. It seems the Pharisees of the day had found a woman in the very act of adultery, which was against Mosaic Law. I love Christ's answer! He bent down beside this woman and on the tile wrote something. I have often wondered what exactly He wrote that day. His writing and Christ's saying, *"...He that is without sin among you, let him first cast a stone at her"* (John 8:7) was enough to move and then remove all of her accusers. Everyone, but Christ and this woman, walked away. To this woman Christ simply said, *"Go...and <u>sin no more</u>."* It was her future, which mattered the most!

We are blessed with a suffering and understanding Savior. We are blessed with a mediator between God our Father and us. We have been given a Christ who knows not only our names, but who suffered for all of our hurtful actions and forgetfulness. Take hold of a hope in Christ. He is our hope – our only chance! My feeling is that it is Christ or it is chaos!

The prophet Isaiah gave a favorite Old Testament scripture regarding error. *"Come now, and let us reason together, saith the Lord: Though your sins be as scarlet, they shall be white as snow; though they be red like crimson, they shall be as wool"* (Isaiah 1:18).

Scarlet, in Isaiah's day, was a dye people thought no one could remove, but Isaiah knew the Lord!

I don't know about you, but to me, sin is the real tragedy in life. I define sin as something done knowingly and pleasurably, which remains unchanged and which hurts yourself and often others around you as well.

I believe that true greatness is measured by how Christ-like we become in this life. Though many disagree, the Bible's James and I believe that simply accepting that there is a Christ is not enough.

We need to plan and put forth a concerted effort to become and do as He is and did. Christ even learned through His suffering (Hebrews 5:8-9). We are wise when we make our bodies follow our God-given spirits!

You don't have to believe me, but the judgment day will come! We will all stand before Christ and report on our thoughts, actions, and words used while here. Many people will then condemn themselves for their unaltered, willful disobedience here in mortality.

Thank goodness there is a way out from under the weights we call sin and death. The way, which Christ provided, we call repentance and resurrection. With a sincere heart and a contrite (humble and teachable) spirit we can overcome completely any sin and all 'bad' effects of mortality - even death. (I think that the sin of pre-meditated murder is in a category of its own).

As a clergyman, when anyone came to me with their head hanging low as the result of some pain they had caused themselves or others, I used to try cheering them a bit by asking, *"You haven't killed anyone have you?"* Fortunately, no one replied, *"Yes!"* Our Savior's own suffering covered whatever error they had fallen into and unfortunately, the world can and does fool us all.

God is a God of mercy. He knows we'll mess up now and then. The God I worship forgives my stupidity. There is always hope!

If you have brought about your own or other's pain, you need to believe the following verses and come to really accept Christ as your personal Save - ior. *"Let the wicked forsake his ways…and he will have mercy upon him…he (God) will* **abundantly** *pardon"* (Isaiah 55:7, word added and emphasized). *"But unto you that fear (respect) my name shall the Sun of righteousness (Christ) arise with* **healing** *in his wings…"* (Malachi 4:2, words and emphasis added).

Because of Christ's suffering and His resurrection we too will each (at least most of us) inherit some kingdom of glory in a similar resurrection one day. We owe him – big time!

Christ will come to this tired, old earth once again, and when He does He will destroy the unsorry and for the truly sorrowful, *"He will swallow up death in victory; and the Lord God will wipe away tears from all faces..."* (Isaiah 25:8).

What a tender tear-wiping time this will be! Not just anyone wipes my tears! I also love the image of Christ with His outstretched, beckoning arms.

Would you abandon your own child in a time of need? Of course not - especially in times of 'trouble'.

Maybe you have said to yourself, *"I just can't endure this goof-up – whatever it may be."*

Norman Vincent Peale personally knew Colonel Sanders (the chicken tycoon), Lucy (of "The I Love Lucy" show), and the athlete who won four gold medals at one Olympic games, Jesse Owens.

Peale said all three successes were at one time questionable. The Colonel was poor, somewhat down on himself, and sixty-five years of age when he began his future chicken empire. Lucy was just a poor New Yorker with a great, positive attitude. And Jesse Owens was a skinny, black Ohioan who once believed that he'd never succeed in life. It was their grit and positiveness, which made all the difference! They never gave up!

I have experienced similar success, although I am not so renowned. I recall vividly, as a grade niner, sitting in a high school awards assembly. A friend, then a senior, received an award for being the school's basketball star. I told myself that one day, despite my five foot six frame, I too would receive this award when a senior. I did, but my grades suffered some. As we think, set goals, and change as necessary we become!

I receive much hope from relatives of ours who lived long ago. Their names were Abraham and Sarah. *"Who against hope believed in hope...*" (Romans 4:18). Abraham was promised a child when one hundred years of age and Sarah had gone into menopause, yet Isaac was born - to them!

When does a true Christian give up? I think never! Remember our Bible's Lazarus who came back from the dead?

Our life really is a test. A test of integrity and there is plenty of pain in this world without us bringing it into or keeping it in our own life and the lives of others.

I used to love a hot summer day and a tough hike in the Rockies. There is nothing quite as refreshing as a cool drink from a mountain stream. God is a lot like this stream. King David says, *"Though I walk in the midst of trouble, thou wilt revive me..."* (Psalm 138:7). I also noticed the Lord say twenty times in Psalms 137, *"...his mercy endureth for ever."*

I'm glad for this! We all make our boo-boos.

A verse I also find helpful in my times of error and forgetfulness is Psalm 119:92, which says, *"Unless thy law had been my delight, I should then have perished in my affliction."*

As previously mentioned, you may feel that, *"What I have or have not done is just too bad, too dirty to be forgiven."* You're wrong! Even in a cyclone there is a quiet, peaceful place. Find it!

Error is always the result of our temporarily forgetting God.

If we are really Christians we must believe we can be forgiven. Bridle yourself in the future, and always remember Him.

Can you tell I like the Psalms? King David knew a great deal about the need for change in his life. Near the beginning of the Psalms this King asks us a question. Next to the much loved and often quoted Psalm 23 are these words I love, *"Who shall ascend into the hill of the Lord? or who shall stand in his holy place? He that hath clean hands (the truly sorry) and has a pure heart (proper desires)..."* (Psalms 24:3,4 words added).

Power, accumulated money, and worldly acknowledgment will mean little if in acquiring these we lose our own integrity – our own souls.

Instead of future pain, may we do better, apologize, and change where necessary as long as we're taking up any position on this diamond.

"Well, I have only fallen down twice so far," I say to myself encouragingly. *"At least I have a good doc.*

Flipping on our T.V. I think, *"And I used to laugh when Steve Erkle said he had fallen and couldn't get up."*

We all unfortunately make mistakes.

Remember, God doesn't care as much about our errors as He cares about what we do about our mistakes in life. Remember, my all time favorite scripture teaches that God is most disappointed in us, His children, when we won't understand and accept His **mercies**.

Write down at least one good, practical idea from this chapter.

_____

_____

Strike Fourteen...
What lasts?

(**M**aybe this is not a strike-maybe it's a ball).
"Well, I made it to the bathroom. The bathroom, yah, let's just say it wasn't pretty! Not that it ever was," I stammer. *"When I reach for this book (the Bible), I don't quite know what it is, but I do feel a bit better today. I just wish it didn't keep getting heavier,"* I say smiling to myself and slinking down into my chair, turning on my vibrating heating pad. *"Let's see, what should I read today? I think I'll read the book of Job. I often wonder how many people have ever read the entire story of Job in one day and realize why he was healed? I surely hadn't. Oh well, here I go again...And there was in the land of Uz..."* I read. *"You just about let me go on without telling you another plus with Ataxia."* I think to myself. *"I'm running out of 'advantages'* and then I realize, *"I can see my dentist, be entirely frozen, and still talk just as well! Bet you can't!"*

What can a person take with them?

No matter what happens or does not happen to you, to really be content in your life you must truly subscribe to the following. King Solomon said these words of wisdom in his proverbs. *"Trust in the Lord with **all** thine heart; and lean not unto thine own understanding. In all thy ways (even in suffering)* *acknowledge him, and he shall direct thy paths"* (Proverb 3:5-6, words and emphasis added).

Unfortunately, most people spend most of their time in life building or collecting monuments to themselves and are 'chasing their own tails' and it is often a hardship that wakes them up.

Often I have compared our lives to a simple journey back home – back to God. We must forget past error and correct where we can and then not worry too much about our past – it's now and our future, which matters the most. When we do our part God will do for us what's best.

I plan on giving away many of my 'things' this Christmas. Not that I plan on leaving soon or anything, but I never use many things I own and they certainly lack the power to bring me peace, well-being, or improved health! I long ago realized that things just do not last.

Certainly we can't take much of this world with us! Or can we?

It's not **if**, but **when** we die? Remember, I've yet to see a hearse with luggage racks!

Scripture often compares mankind to grass or stubble, which is quickly consumed. I have seen prairie fires and helped my grandpa burn grass off his hillside so I know what a 'nothing' our worldly possessions are. Poof!

The Bible makes me believe that even our earth must suffer and die – I'm pretty sure global warming is real!

It's natural to wonder how long you must endure your particular pain. The answer, though tough, is to the 'end' – the bottom of the ninth inning whatever that might entail.

Instead of thinking that at least some of life has been good to you, realize that all along – even now - it has been a loving God who has been good to you!

While on this earth there is one thing most essential to your peace – your sincere trust in God! *"Some trust in chariots,*

and some in horses: but we will remember the Lord our God"
(Psalms 20:7).

Certainly, you wouldn't have picked your unique pain, but it is how you respond that counts the most!

Since our health trial I have often thought, *"Do we really believe what we say we believe?"* Trials and time will tell.

As a student teacher I once taught a grade 11 Social Studies class in a private all Christian high school. Many of these students had some great values!

I had just arrived home from my own Christian mission in Japan. At this school part of a student's daily routine was to receive an hour of religious instruction. You can imagine my surprise and happiness when the religion teacher invited me to tell the kids a bit about my beliefs.

I decided to speak about what my faith says really lasts. The kids agreed that even though our wedding vows often include 'till death do us part' they believed **relationships** could last forever. I don't know about you, but I just can't accept any God who does not continue our families. To me heaven just wouldn't be heaven without those we love. I want no vacant seats at the table in heaven.

These students were also taught that day that they could have a real relationship with God too.

They were told that we, of course, continue to live even after our mortal lives have ended. And, they were told that despite a big part of life might involve suffering and though they may be told that this life is not fair, in the end it will be even more than just and fair!

We also concluded that day that our **knowledge** (wisdom and experience) could go with us.

After I had fielded a few questions the regular teacher and I talked alone. He did not believe in a life after death (the resurrection) and he said Christ's miracles were not real – but symbolic. He didn't even believe in the resurrection. I couldn't have disagreed more! In the end we agreed to disagree, but I felt a bit sorry for this teacher – and those students.

Besides the living again of our bodies and spirits, and the important relationships we develop, I believe that there is not a whole lot more that we can take along.

Another favorite modern movie of mine is "The Guardian" with Kevin Costner and Ashton Kutcher. This is a 'must see' movie (and I don't recommend many movies these days). At the movie's close, you will see one of the things that can really last! I suppose this is why I enjoyed this show so much.

A young newly wed died awhile back and a grandpa said, *"I just can't believe in a God who allows this!"* Yes, some mistakenly, as difficult as death can be, think there should be no suffering at all in this world.

Our eldest son and wife just had a perfectly formed baby boy. What a marvel! It's when I see a newborn child that I most feel that there indeed is a Supreme Creator.

Yet, no babies come without some suffering. It's just part of this existence. We also recently had a young family we know 'lose' their infant son.

How does one explain the SIDS baby, a child born in a gutter, or with Down's syndrome, or the abused?

Once again, I believe that God allows suffering for His children to fully experience a small bit of Christ's suffering. Yet, many just shrug their shoulders and say," *Well, life's just not fair!"*

In my opinion, we all need to accept that suffering is a natural part of life. *"(we learn)…precept upon precept; line upon line…here a little, and there a little…and fall backward, (are) broken, and snared, and taken"* (Isaiah 28:9,13, word added). God teaches us the most through suffering and some suffering is supposed to take place in each of our lives.

I'm not completely certain who wrote Hebrews, but I am convinced that some of our most helpful verses of truth lie within these pages. Did you realize that there is no trouble

that Christ has not felt and that He cannot help us with? *"…
he himself hath suffered being tempted (tried), he is able to succor
(sustain) them that are tempted"* (Hebrews 2:18, words added).

The best anyone can do sometimes is to do as my dad
counseled and just <u>carry on</u>, so I encourage you all to hang
on and suffer as best you can with dignity. No one needs a
complainer. Have no fear except fear of being a coward.

We chose this life! The Bible even says we spirits fought
a war and won our right to mortality and to our present
suffering. I often have wondered what kind of war we fought
as spirits? *"And there was war in heaven, Michael (Adam) and his
angels (spirits) fought against the dragon (Satan)…"* (Revelation
12:7, words added). Can you believe it? We chose this?

We are choosers of – agents who largely decide how we
respond to our outside influences – suffering included!

To teach us that we lived before our mortality, even the
Pharisees of Christ's time believed in our former existence.
Christ himself taught, *"And his disciples asked him, saying,
Master, who did sin, the man, or his parents, that he was born blind"*
(John 9:2)?

Christ's answer is what really matters. He responded in
verse ten, *"Jesus answered, neither…"* (John 9:3).

I believe that God himself must operate by laws (like
condensation) and one of those natural laws is that we will
all have opposition in this life.

We must accept this inevitability and in today's vernacular
'suck it up'! We too must eventually 'be weaned' and even
maybe 'provoked' into believing and accepting Christ.

I re-realized this when a long time friend called me as he
approached death's door. He said, in essence, *"I was never much
of a church-goer in this life, but I want you to know I believe that I
will meet God again."*

Some, teaching their version of truth, misguide us. Think
for yourself.

The one Bible teaching that really helps me more than any other is by John. He says that," *In my Father's house are many mansions (there's even a place for me): if it were not so, I would have told you...*" (John 14:2, words added).

My wife once asked, *"Would you really not go back to how things were before this sickness?"* My answer was, *"No! Do not judge the inside by what may be on the outside. However, there are days..."*

It is the suffering Christ, who in His at-one-ment made it possible for mankind to bravely endure our difficulties – that makes us all sufferers one with Christ (I know that anything we suffer can hardly be compared with Christ's)!

To me, God is good – **always** - and one of our major purposes in mortality is to learn to endure well our physical and emotional aches, pains, and bruises because we are hopefully learning to act more like him.

So, what does a person take with them? What really lasts?

I repeat, we all have come into this life to gain experience (memories) and Godly knowledge. These we take with us as well as earthly and Godly relationships if we so live. And, believe it or not (and I'm not boasting), I expect to have a place set for me, but yes, there's work to be done here.

Really think about Jesus Christ a minute. He went into Jerusalem knowing full well His own upcoming pain, yet he went. What a man! What a hero to emulate! He sure must love us!

Part of the really good news of the gospel of Jesus Christ is that, with help from Christ, we can endure some crawling, mental and physical challenges, loss of privacy, death, and all the pains that this old world and it's people seems to 'dish out'.

In my opinion too many preach of a better world, but few actually back those words with their actions. If you want to know if someone is really committed to helping the suffering, then call upon his or her wallet. God and people blessed with money get things done!

Stocks crashed in 1929. The U.S. banks went under in 1933. In the 2000's there continues to be economic challenges all over this globe.

The 'dirty thirties' caused many people severe drought, hunger, and personal destitution.

WWI and WWII transpired and now over sixty years later we often feel unsafe? Country leaders seem to pursue their 'own' atomic weapon more than they pursue people's peace. Has life gone amok?

In a very real sense I predict a time of difficulty for our world. I do not wish to sound gloomy, but here's what the Prophet Daniel said, speaking of the last days – our days. *"At that time (today) shall Michael stand up…and there shall be a time of trouble, such as never was since there was a nation…"* (Daniel 12:1, words added).

I have often pondered the supreme power – God.

The story is told of an inexperienced hunter who hired an old Native guide. In the morning the guide had disappeared. When the hunter followed his guide's footsteps in the lightly fallen snow he found him in a wooded area praying.

Our hunter never prayed. In fact, he claimed there was no God, but out of respect for his guide he waited quietly for his prayer to conclude.

After some intense questioning by the hunter as to why the guide wasted his time praying and realizing his hunter friend had followed his footprints in the freshly fallen snow the wise old guide responded, while pointing at the now rising sun, *"Behold the footprints of God."*

If we will be wise and follow Christ and God His Father we will never go astray – even and especially when we 'die'! We will live again and if we've strayed we can come back! That's the really good news. These are the *"good tidings of great joy"*.

I'm afraid that instead of fully recognizing and appreciating God's many creations, people's hearts are focused elsewhere, their ears don't hear well the things of God and their eyes are somewhat dimmed.

Do you take time to really marvel at God's creations? If so, please explain why some are self-declared atheists – take a look at what puny man can make. Why do some think of suicide (you who are battling depressions may be partially exempted – keep fighting)?

A suffering friend and I were sharing our challenging states just the other day. I asked him, *"If a hardship brings you closer to God, is it really a hardship or a well-disguised blessing?"*

God has allowed suffering to come into our world. Our challenge is not purposeless. Like a goldsmith's refining fire, the heat is turned up now and then. If not so, **all** is dross.

The inward part of you that knows of God's love must be fed or it too can and will die – especially during difficult times. Read about Christ! By your suffering you are learning life's truly essential lessons.

If you profess to be a Christian, of any denomination, you accept that Jesus Christ overcame all suffering – even death – and you must agree that when this mortality ends, for sure there will be more.

Reading from the Bible each day has truly brought me a measure of comfort. I am confident it can help you navigate your day as well.

A Country singer tells of just weeks to live. Our sick, soon to die cowboy rides a bull named *"Fumanchu"* and does many other fun things, but he also reads his Bible – for his very first time. Don't wait until then!

My parents taught me to love and it has always been easy for me to see the goodness in other people. We're all just plodding along – trying to do a bit better. A trial might well be the time for some to make final preparations to meet God! It's not scary when you really trust.

Mother Teresa used to run into the middle of war zones and riots in order to help people. When being formally interviewed (which she avoided like the plague – wait a minute, even a plague never stopped her) she was asked, *"Aren't you afraid when you run into the middle of a war or a riot?"* I love her answer. This petite, little nun replied with a question of her own. She queried, *"What? Am I supposed to be afraid of meeting God?"*

Remember, it was not raining when Noah built his ark and so my advice applies not only to the suffering, but to us all today!

The Apostle Paul suffered lashings, imprisonment, shipwrecks and more, yet he never wavered.

Before our toe tagging and ring removing experience, let's learn life's most important lessons and spend some time helping all who have suffered or who now suffer in any way. Let's especially accept Christ!

It might sound strange, but you may not trade your current form of suffering because of what you are becoming.

Don't lose heart! Speaking about Christ, Paul says, *"By whom also we have access…we glory in tribulations also; knowing that tribulation worketh patience (it certainly does)"* (Romans 5: 2-5, words added).

My prayer for you is this…may you confront whatever hardship comes your way. May you 'take it like a man?'(Having witnessed my wife bare our five children, maybe I should say may you; 'take it like a woman')!

Job says, *"I would seek unto God, and unto God would I commit my cause"* (Job 5:8).

If your attitude is God-like, in time we may actually 'rejoice' in our suffering. *"My son, (remember, you are his unforgotten child) despise thou not the chastening of the Lord…For whom the Lord loveth he chasteneth (strange way to show love)… But if ye be without chastisement (for a while) then ye are…not sons"* (Hebrews 12:5-8, words added).

Read these verses to see yourself what the unaccepting of difficulty will become. Paul used some pretty graphic wording to make his point!

One day people will read an obituary telling of your death. Please, don't fully believe this. You are forever! I used to tell our kids that they have two dads – one is their Heavenly Father (God) and the other is me!

Sure, there are some things I try to alter, but oh well, for now.

I remember being outside building our house when Washington's, Mt. Saint Helen erupted in the 1980s. For some time, though living in a completely different country, my vision was obscured.

In living we can't afford to have our vision obscured very long! We need to focus on what matters the most. My dad often said to me, "*In life, a person isn't allowed too many mistakes.*"

<u>Hope against hope</u> (Romans 4) and realize that what Christ himself promises is true! The great prophet Isaiah had it figured out when he said, "*... it is written, "Eye hath not seen, nor ear heard, neither have entered into the heart of man, the things which God hath prepared for them that love him*" (1 Corinthians 2:9).

So, when do we Christians give up? We don't because we will live forever!

Some people think that focusing life on Christ is crazy or weak. Not me! Faith has been called by many unbelievers, 'opium for the weak'. Nevertheless, I know a God who is literally our Father. I know He sent his Only Begotten Son (Christ) to die for us **all**. And, I know Jesus Christ can still speak and comfort us today through His Holy Spirit – if we'll but listen to Him and have room and time for Him in our inns.

Should I tell you my vision of heaven? There will be no suffering there, many family and friends will greet us near a gate, roads will be paved with gold, and of course there will be an indescribably beautiful baseball stadium!

I was once at a baseball clinic with a son. Former Yankees were there when Brian Doyle, a 400 hitter in the 1978 World Series, signed our son's baseball like this – Joshua 1:8. *"This book of the law…thou shalt meditate therein day and night…***then** *thou shalt have good success."*

Brian Doyle understood what really lasted in life and it wasn't his hitting abilities. His life was based firmly on the word of God.

Often in our Bible Christ himself is referred to as 'The Word'. We'd do well to give Christ the final word in our lives! The Word is all-powerful. I have seen Him change lives.

In our times of crisis, our money and position will suddenly, and often surprisingly, mean nothing. May we turn to God before that day comes?

At funerals I often enjoyed sharing a version of the following. Apparently, former U. S. President, John Quincy Adams, was hobbling along some street in Boston when a dear friend encountered him. *"How are you?"* his friend asked.

John Quincy's response was classic. He answered something like, *" My house is rather sorely dilapidated and I think I will soon be leaving it behind, but John – John Quincy Adams is just fine, thank you!"*

A dear friend just returned from a road trip through much of the western coastal United States. As he drove he noticed a sign in a small, country store, which said in effect that a stream only gurgles because it encounters rocks.

In my life I have found that at times the 'veil' between this life and the next has been very thin.

There was my first exposure to this somewhat unexplainable phenomenon when just a boy. My dad had almost finished conducting a future missionary's farewell church service. Dad never lied, yet after careful contemplation, turning and looking at this future missionary, Dad boldly told this missionary that he had seen – yes **seen** – the boy's recently deceased grandpa, among the audience. Of course many scoffed – especially a woman who had recently said goodbye to her own husband.

In those days one traveled to church leaders far away to have hands laid on your head to officially become a missionary. A relative of David Tanner's, acted as voice. You can just imagine the look on people's faces in our small town when they were informed that Nathan, this man, who knew of E. P.'s death, told David that his Grandpa Tanner had attended his mission farewell.

There was also the day I became a congregation's chief clergyman – a Bishop. I was about to speak to a rather large audience, when my predecessor, a man I admire, leaned over to me and pointing to a bench near the rear of our chapel said, *"See just over there, that is where I saw your dad sitting one Sunday."* Dad had been 'gone' many years then.

As clergy I was often privileged beyond description to remain present at a loved one's 'death'. They often spoke to or saw people and things unexplainable by human lips.

Yes, you may say, *"It's the drugs,"* but I feel there is more! I view death as a mere part of life we all must face. To me, death is like the horseback rider who rides away into the nearby foothills - or the ship whose sails disappear into the horizon. We may no longer see him or the ship, but that certainly does not mean they no longer exist! I believe others are saying, *"Hello!"*

God, our Father, and His Son will be there along with other loved ones from this life who have tried to meet God's conditions and treated others respectfully while here on earth. We will greet loved ones there. This is only rational. Truth and reason go hand in hand!

I view death as Norman Peale viewed dying. He often told what he referred to as "The Parable of the Unborn Child". Just as the unborn infant is comfortable in his home inside his or her mother's womb, the day comes when that child must leave to grow. He or she must 'be born' or so we call it. We think this is quite natural. In time, we come to love people and our surroundings here on earth. We are comfortable. Yet, our day comes and we must be 're-born'. We call this rebirth or transition our death.

You don't have to believe me. Can you explain completely the miracle inventions of our day – a computer, for example? I sure can't!

And how does a ram of power work? Or how can one person stand, talk into a microphone, and be heard around the globe? Like most of us, there's sure a lot I don't understand. Much I do by faith.

We just returned from a graveside ceremony for a high school friend of mine. This got me really thinking about what lasts.

The objective in baseball is to score more runs than your opponent. Isn't it ironic that the objective in life is to help 'the other guy' score?

I remember those center field chats whenever our opponent was victorious. I will never forget my coach's final words as tears coursed down many childish cheeks, *"Remember, it's only a game!"*

"Think I better have my nap," I say as our doorbell rings. *"A good, young friend just stopped by. He will be going out on a Christian mission soon – trying as best he can to make this world a better place! Good for him,"* I say to myself, as our front door gently closes, *"And I used to be his school teacher. Nice of him to visit an older guy like me!"* I may be staying home, but I think I too have a mission (job) to accomplish."* With a gleam in my eye, I return to my reading chair to learn a bit more. *"My ignorance*

is so profound!" I mutter to myself. *"Not to discourage anyone, but it seems that the more I learn, the more I realize that I have much to learn. Maybe now that I am sick and without an employer I can understand just a little bit more – especially of people's pains."* Suddenly, our CD player shuts off and the words, *"See you"* show on the display. Today marks an all-time high (or low depending how you look at it) as I talked back to the **machine** saying, *"See you too!"*

Think about it. What can you take when you die?

Write down at least one helpful idea to remember from this chapter.

_____

_____

Strike Fifteen…
Life Lessons Learned from Baseball

" *I just love baseball as I'm sure you can tell! It's game One of the World Series tonight,"* I think to myself as I rub my hands together. *"Wonder if you like baseball too? You know, whoever invented this game should have a seat in heaven,"* I think and I smile! *" Here are just a few things about ordinary me and lessons I learned from my years in Little League Baseball. These life lessons serve me well and may help you too! If baseball isn't your thing, don't worry, this chapter won't talk too much baseball. But then, is that even possible? Oh yah!"* I remember, *" an 'advantage' of our disease. Well, one plus is that I can still type. Wait a second, maybe my readers won't agree? Oh well. The real 'good' thing is that at least a former Yankee named Lou Gehrig had ALS and my disease is a cousin. So, if we have an illness, at least it's a baseball sickness. It's also amazing what a better listener I'm gradually becoming too (men aren't too good at this). It helps when you're no longer able to talk so much or walk away!"*

So, thanks for spending a few hours with an old, suffering baseball fan like me. I promised these readings would add value to your life and make your experience here on our planet more understandable and more bearable. I hope that I have said something that helps you through your suffering.

These writings gave me some meaningful work to do each day. May your suffering be more understandable because you took this time to share with me.

Dad used to say, *"Every man and woman has a story to tell."* I have since decided that he was right – and each story is well worth hearing! I wish I knew yours!

This last chapter is about an average guy and his growing up years playing baseball, and striking out or being rained out a few times, and initially, unwisely buying into the idea that sometimes, *"Life's not fair."*

In time, I came to realize that life would be more than fair – if I would just keep playing until the game ended. I have also learned that we can actually do some things about 'games' we play to make them more bearable right now!

Anyone who really understands me knows that faith and family come way before any sport – even baseball! Yet, I have learned things from sports so I framed this book and stories within the context of strategies we can all use as we take on life.

Twenty years ago today I said my final goodbye in this life to my dad and coach. He taught me some great lessons. My dad would say things like (and I know I said this earlier, but… *"Winning isn't everything, wanting to win fairly is!"*

Before any game of baseball there is a warm up. Before earth life we have to have had some kind of warm up (existence) too, cause here we are playing now and you sure don't create something from nothing!

Some may disagree, but your 'being on the field' now is no accident. We inherited our particular field, time, and our teams and we ought to feel blessed to have such opportunities and teammates.

Let me state how big a fan I also am of Socrates. He was the father, many believe, of modern ethics and was willing to give his life for what he believed. Socrates (and I agree) said that there was only one thing he was really sure of and that was his own ignorance. Socrates, like Plato, also believed that critical thought was an essential part of a meaningful life.

When arraigned in a court for 'corrupting youth' (he felt he had been called of God to teach) he mocked the judge by suggesting that he ought to simply be fined a small amount of money and then released. They say he was sentenced to drink hemlock and die.

Despite my own ignorance I did learn some things about life from Little League Baseball and in closing, these principles may help you too!

1ˢᵗ inning and Life Lesson #1- "If the ball is hit to you, know in advance where you'll throw it."

Sometimes we are blind-sided in life, but usually we can see challenges coming and can do something in advance to avoid or better entrap them. However, there are exceptions!

Once I was cutting the weeds along a ditch on my grandpa's farm. I sat on the metal chair attached to a long cutting arm and we were pulled by my grandpa's old, John Deere tractor. Suddenly, we hit an anthill. Though I can't recall much of the ensuing moments, I found myself helplessly flailing through the air, landing kettle over teapot somewhere in the long, prairie grass. Surprise!

As you can imagine, these events completely surprised everyone – especially my unsuspecting grandpa and the ants! Our lives can be like this, like the bounces of a baseball – surprising!

Hopefully, days like the misfortune described above are few and far between if not non-existent! Yet, even though 'stuff' happens, having an idea of where you'll 'throw the ball' if it comes your way is wise advice.

We all have a beginning in life, and in many ways they are the same – here's how mine was unique.

I've been told I was born on a beautiful, Saturday afternoon. I have often since thought - a great time for a doubleheader.

Though I must confess that I do not personally remember, Mom says I looked so much like a Native Canadian baby that my attending nurse put a feather in my long, dark hair and placed me in a crib.

Mom says of this day that she had to hurry to deliver me so my friend, Bob, could be born at 12:30 PM. Perhaps this is why, all my life, I have rather resented feeling hurried?

Things sure change. Bob recently visited to inform me personally of his cancer (he has since gone ahead), and my family has to care for me in my current state.

As before mentioned, dad was my coach. He was a center fielder and clean-up batter in his day. WWII and age got in the way of a possible career in baseball. Mom says he once even tried out for the Los Angeles Dodgers. He was just too old. At least that's Mom's story so I'm sticking to it!

I soon realized that where a Little League shortstop threw the ball depended on many factors. There was which side I fielded the ball, what type of hit was made, what bases were occupied, and then there was the evaluation of a fellow player's attentiveness etc. These decisions had to be made instantly when hit the ball. Thinking and deciding ahead really helped.

More than once I recall a teammate being lackadaisical and not watching the ball at all times. The player was hit in the face with the ball as coach yelled out, *"Where's the play?"*

Being the third child of six, I found myself between an older brother, Wade, an older sister, Diane, and three younger sisters, Marianne, Mona, and Karen.

Childhood in the 50s had its wonderful times and I began playing games. There was, 'Auntie I Over', 'Frozen Tag', the dreaded 'Kiss, Kiss, or Torture', and my favorite – baseball!

All Wade's larger-than-life friends were at the diamond so how could I not fall in love for my very first time?

At an unusually early age I had learned to throw straight by playing catch with our wheelchair bound scorekeeper – an experience I now cherish more as I find myself in such a chair with someone graciously helping me in and out of a car.

I recall how badly I felt when I accidentally hit my catch partner in the legs. He'd always say, *"It didn't hurt,"* but I felt it!

I suppose my sense of responsibility grew too as I soon understood that if I threw wildly, **I** had to chase the ball. Thinking ahead and knowing that actions held a consequence helped me better play all games.

Though simply the batboy, being too young to play myself, I was sure that this was **my** team.

In life we all get unexpected 'curve balls', 'change ups', and 'bad hops' now and then. My dad taught me to look ahead. In life, like baseball, let's not be too short sighted – look optimistically ahead. Position and brace yourself as best you can and prepare for whatever comes your way.

2nd Inning and life Lesson #2 – "Don't give too much heed to your fears."

A California friend of mine was recently scraping the 1970s style white stipple from his ceiling with a razor blade. A few blades somehow accidentally made their way into his shoe.

Now passing through an airport the freeloading razors were detected by an X-ray and my buddy was in a pickle. Though unexpected, the worst thing he could do is fear – he was innocent! I have since thought to myself, *"Good thing at least they didn't taser him."*

My coach (my Dad) had served the Canadian Navy in WWII. There he had faced many life threatening waves and torpedo laden enemy ships on his thirteen trips across the

North Atlantic, so I guess he thought it was time for his 1954-born son to face a little opposition of his own.

In a big game, Pop put me in! At the tender age of eight I faced a much older and stronger pitcher – later in life he was to become Canada's basketball Olympic team captain.

My uniform was dragging in the dirt while the pitcher's uniform didn't cover his knees. Good thing I was so much shorter than he was – I walked! Terrifying!

I soon realized the real enemy at bat (and in life) is fear. Maybe that is why I cheered inside when a son of ours was hit by a ball twice in the same eye and still wanted to play catch – learn to live in the moment!

This was when I first began thinking that things do not just happen for no reason (trials too) – they are there purposely to teach us important life lessons - if we'll listen and just not fear. We are really not in control of much of life.

You may have your own 'pitchers' and you may feel out sized and overwhelmed, but you can overcome.

I am reminded of a person Dad talked about many years ago. It was from the Bible. The man's name was David. Goliath was pitching that day (1 Samuel 17). Against all odds little David defeated this giant. You must face your own fears. David, though a frightened army looked on, was really, for the most part, on his own that day – just he, his God, and some trust.

Roosevelt was right when he said of his enemy that what his team had to fear most was fear itself.

I'm not proud that the crowds boo a lot in baseball, but I have learned that it's when they boo the loudest (in times of opposition) that heroes have the chance to be born. This may well be your chance to hit a 'homerun'.

Our extended family is pretty ordinary, but we have faced cancer, disability, divorce, death, and more! Know what? The 'game goes on' and all along our most divisive enemy has been our own fear. Job said, *"At destruction and famine thou shalt laugh: neither shalt thou be afraid of the beasts of the field."* (Job 5:22).

Even the famous Babe Ruth would often strike out; in fact, they say he held several records. One was for the most strikeouts in a single season, but this didn't stop him from becoming a homerun king.

In my first book I tell about the day I was accomplice to burning down a barn – I know, I should have been playing baseball. It is true about the fire; at a very innocent age my cousin and I accidentally torched a neighbor's chicken coop – oops! We promptly went swimming. I remember my fear of coming home was far worse than any punishment parents actually gave me. I sincerely apologized to my neighbor and that was pretty much that. So, let's not give too much heed to our fears – face them instead!

I will never forget the day a son and daughter-in-law sat me down in the living room and used the c-word – cancer!

Some days certainly are more memorable than others, but please don't fear!

3rd Inning and Life Lesson # 3 – "Life does have its unexpected surprises."

The baseball story is told of two 90-year-old men, Howard and Greg. They had been close baseball buddies all of their lives.

Greg was dying so Howard visited him every day.

One day Howard said, *"Greg, we both loved baseball all our lives. When you get to heaven, let me know if there's baseball up there will you?"*

Greg looked up at Howard from his deathbed, *"Howard, you've been my best bud for many years. I'll do this if possible!"*

Greg soon passed away.

A few nights later, Howard was awakened by a bright light and a voice calling, *"Howard--Howard."*

"Who is it?" asked Howard.

"It's me, Greg."

"It can't be, Greg just died," Howard responded.

"Really, it's me, Greg," insisted the voice.

"Greg! Where are you?"

"In heaven!" replies Greg. *"I have some really good news and a little bad news."*

"Tell me the good news first," says Howard.

"The good news," Greg says," *is that there is baseball in heaven and the backstops are made of gold. Better yet, all of our old buddies who died before us are here, too and we're all so honest that we need no umps. We're all young again like the guys in the baseball movie, "Field of Dreams". It's always light, and we can play baseball all we want."*

"That's fantastic," said Howard. *"So what could possibly be the bad news?"*

"You're scheduled to pitch Tuesday."

There are a few surprises in our lives!

While watching baseball we love eating a box of cracker jacks. I don't know exactly what it is, but a box of the stuff just seems to make a baseball game even more perfect. The box always contained some cheesy surprise and I have come to see that life, like baseball snacks, often holds a few 'treats' as well.

An old preacher, trying to teach his lesson more effectively, is said to have placed four empty transparent glass cups on his podium. He put alcohol in the first glass, a lit cigarette in the second, chocolate syrup in his third glass, and clean, rich topsoil in the last. Into each jar he carefully placed a worm and waited. Soon the first three worms died with only the top soiled worm surviving. The old fellow then had his surprise. He asked the congregation what they had learned from this (not a wise idea). Just imagine the look on his face as his young, teenage parishioner replied, *"If we drink, smoke, and eat chocolate we will never die of worms!"* Surprise!

As a very young child, I swore I would never steal. And, now here was **my dad** teaching six to twelve year olds how to 'steal' bases. I believed that was wrong to steal anything and I still recall my confusion, but I got over it.

School years came and went with the majority of my teachers being my relations, which in my estimation, besides sports, was the best thing about school.

A teacher hooked me and some friends on basketball in grade six and we trounced an opposing team. The 'Purple People Eaters' were okay for winter, but baseball remained my true passion.

Speaking of surprises, I'm pretty sure I once owned a Mickey Mantle card and my best baseball buddy, Roger, owned a Roger Maris card too, but – surprise – we traded them away! Accept the unexpected.

These were innocent days - days when teachers still played afternoon World Series radio games over the school's loudspeaker. Days when children could see most games, as night games were yet to be invented.

In my future I'd become a better teacher myself because of the baseball-on-radio lesson by my grandma, the Oriole fan, had given me.

Junior and senior high are pretty much a blur – the 60s and 70s were mainly about basketball or baseball. I was never inclined to be too rude, mean, or rebellious, but I do recall one error.

Lila ran a confectionary and since being grade four classmates, and learning some English together, this Chinese war bride and I had been close friends. This didn't stop me from stealing chocolate bars from her though. I guess I learned my stealing lesson well – maybe too well!

I wrote Lila an apology and sent her more than enough money in the mail before becoming a Christian missionary in

Tokyo, Japan. I felt a bit guilty and I really should have talked to her.

Imagine my surprise, upon my return, at meeting her only to have her tell me of this money-receiving incident and then have her wrongfully accuse my good friend. Life does have its share of unanticipated surprise endings.

4th inning and Life Lesson #4- " Dependability and hard work matter."

Money was fairly important back then so my careers at work began. This was before our current burger-flipping-generation jobs even existed.

I will never forget my first job – I was batboy so it was my job to care for all the equipment. *"Yes!"*

At age 11, I stacked hay bales with my boss. He actually trusted me enough to drive his steering wheel mounted 'standard' pickup truck around his field and I began learning that life, like a haystack or a good baseball game, is a lot of sweat and hard work.

I soon ended up stacking bales with friends. We'd take a wooden case of Cola (24 pop) and put it in the nearby cool creek before starting.

Lunches were not to be forgotten. I don't know how many haystacks we made, but the home cooked, country meals I'll never forget!

Other jobs were interspersed with eating sunflower seeds (a baseball thing to do) at the old swimming pool or while sitting on a local confectionary's 'bum bench' and other jobs included pounding fence posts for our county, painting grain elevators, working at a local canning factory, in window and door assembly lines etc.

Though many of my jobs were outside, it was mostly from baseball that I learned it is good for both body and spirit to spend as much time out-of-doors as possible.

Much of a hot, sunny day or job, like a baseball game – like living - was grunt work and sweat, but the game was always well worth struggling over.

5th inning and Life Lesson #5 – <u>"Make the underdog a part of your life!"</u>

The sooner we learn that there is as much dignity in being a batboy as in being star of the game the better.

Stand up for the underdog!

Sleeping over at what I determined then to be an 'under-privileged' friend's home or standing up for the poor high school aged girl with her potato sandwich just seemed natural to me and I'm so glad I did. Though imperfect (in an elementary school class picture I did cut out the photo of a girl who had 'fleas') I almost always favored the 'picked on'.

I recall a younger friend telling me how much standing up for her had meant at the time.

In the game of baseball there is always the kid at the plate who is scared to death. Life can be this way and my heart still goes out for such a batter or anyone living in fear.

Some of my best memories of baseball center around the underdog. I'll never forget the poor, fatherless boy without a glove of his own. Help them! It's one of a happy game's hints.

It seems to me like some are just gifted when it comes to baseball. Some people are born with a 'canon' for an arm and others seem to have a knack at hitting that round ball with that round bat.

I was always just average when it came to my arm and bat. Maybe that's why I always favored the team that everyone else picked as loser – except for the Yankees that is.

As I look back I now realize that few players were ever talented enough to 'get it all right'. There are plenty of errors in almost any game. Forget them and stay in the game.

Thank heavens for the average and the underdog – the worker and sweater. There would not be much of a game without them!

6th and final inning and Life Lesson #6 – "It ain't over till it's over!"

My Little League team was once 27 runs behind our more talented opponent in our last at bats. We won!

The Yankees catcher, Yogi Berra, was right when he said, *"It ain't over till it's over."*

Remember the Kirk Gibson homerun? It was the 1988 World Series. Gibson had hurt both knees in the National League championship and was not expected to even pinch hit. Trailing in game one by a score of 4-3 for Oakland, and with one man on base, you can imagine Kirk's surprise when the manager, Tommy Lasorda, called him up. With two out, two strikes against him, two bad legs, and hitting against the future hall of famer, Dennis Eckersley, Kirk swung just once winning with his homer. My brother even called me within minutes as he watched from Ottawa. They say many unbelieving Dodger fan's taillights could be seen as the ball silently sailed over the right field fence.

Yes, life can be ironic! You may not see any hope, but there may just be a door you haven't tried – keep trying!

Let's be glad we're alive despite our hardships. Most of us can still at least show love, play, sit at a playground, or look up at the stars.

We must get to that place where we accept no falsehoods, do away with selfishness, and fear nothing – absolutely nothing! King David once said, though you may not feel this way now, *"It is good for me that I have been afflicted: that I might learn thy statutes"* (Psalms 119:71).

Umpires do make wrong calls and at first glance life may seem unfair too. One of the great truths is that life is hard, but as said before, I trust that in the final inning it will be more than fair! In the end everyone will bat evenly so just keep trying to win and you will!

God doesn't view life's pitches the same way we all too often do – many of us have more challenges than others. Thinking like God thinks is essential to ever receiving any measure of comfort. *"For my thoughts are not your thoughts, neither are your ways my ways, saith the Lord. For as the heavens are higher than the earth, so are my ways higher than your ways, and my thoughts than your thoughts."* (Isaiah 55:8,9)

Learn to think like God and just 'keep swinging'.

In social studies I used to teach about China. I would put on an unusually large pair of glasses and then explain to the students that to really understand Orientals, you must begin to see this world from their perspective.

For example, in much of North America we view a nice lawn as an essential. In most of Asia, a nice lawn is nothing but a huge waste of potential food producing land. The same is so with your sickness or any other trial – learn to view life as God does.

Dad used to yell, *"Keep your eye on the ball!"* In all of life I say, *"Keep your eye on God to the end and remember that there is no end. God never gives up!"*

I think to myself, *"Will these lessons learned really help anyone?"* Then I realize, *"If just one lesson helps even one suffering person through the day, I've been paid plenty. To which charity will I give the proceeds from this book?"* I wonder. Then I have it! *"Of course! I'll put night-lights on at least one of our local baseball diamonds and buy the children some new uniforms! Then I'll give any other profits to our local baseball teams. I certainly don't need or even want the money anymore! Seems like many people spend*

most of their health acquiring wealth and then they spend most of their wealth on health. Ironic!"

Write down at least one idea from this chapter, which you will now use.

_____

_____

Epilogue

Can we really trust God?

We will all suffer one way or another in mortality – that's just life so don't take our struggles or ourselves too seriously. You know, we're one person living in this Milky Way and they say there are 200 billion stars (burning suns) within our one galaxy alone and astrologers know of over 200 billion galaxies. May we all place our challenges within their proper perspective. Knowing this about the stars helps me put myself and my struggles and strikeouts into perspective. How about you?

I love what Christ says in the Bible regarding suffering and even seemingly unjust suffering. He said, *"...but if, when ye do well, and suffer for it patiently, this is acceptable with God.... Christ also suffered for us, leaving us an example, that we should follow his steps"* (1 Peter 20-21).

As we suffer in life we all owe much to others and to God. For many of us there are professionals, parents, or dear friends who have helped or are now helping us along our way. Let's be grateful for them!

I long ago decided that a person's true character is seldom revealed in times of peace and prosperity, but rather in times of turmoil and trial.

I love 2 Corinthians 3:2-3 which says, *"Ye are our epistle... written not in ink, but with the spirit of the living God: not in tablets of stone, but in fleshy tablets of the heart."*

Your time of struggle may be your time to show a proper example for others to follow – to be that 'fleshy heart'. This may be your time to 'be someone for someone else'.

Too often when difficulty strikes a life, a person reacts instead of acting. In all challenges be real, but don't allow your realness to lead to endless complaints. My mom just gave me an awesome book to read. It's called "A Complaint Free World." Just imagine such a place. As tough as this may be, act thankfully! May you 'live' throughout your adversity?

We have discussed just a few ways we may suffer in this crazy, pain-filled, and yet purposeful life. In whatever conditions you may find yourself remember the wise council Apostle Paul once gave, *"...I (Paul) have learned, in whatsoever state I am, therewith to be content"* (Philippians 4:11, word added).

As hard as life can be, I'm convinced that God knows best! Does He make mistakes? I don't think so.

I believe we have a God who runs this thing we call life. God loves all people because of who He is – our Father! And because we are His and He loves us He sent us His Only Begotten Son. You can endure anything through Christ, who can strengthen you. I truly do believe, *"I (you too!) can do all things through Christ which strengtheneth me"* (Philippians 4:13, words added). Paul said 'all' things! This verse was the favorite of one of our recent U.S. presidential candidates.

There are many good churches out there and many good, honest people of all faiths. My hope is that by your reading this book you at least have gotten some comfort and made some sense of your own suffering.

I certainly don't have the answer to all of life's challenges, but I do know we are better off if we take time to marvel at nature, get up early enough to be silent (listen for God), and we give thanks for what is 'right' in our lives.

Affliction, with its many stern faces, helps us learn the tough lessons in life that we would have otherwise likely failed to have learned. Because of suffering we will never be the same – we'll be better!

From this point on we will view our suffering differently (renewed in mind)! Hardship will now become a turning point rather that a stop sign. Today forward we will no longer view life as a big playground, but more as a classroom and a teacher with some very difficult lessons to be learned. Those currently facing trial or acting as caregivers have been invited into class. Others await their invitation. Now, that's real life!

"And be not conformed to this world: but be ye transformed by the renewing of your mind..." (Romans 12:2).

In his autobiography, on page 198, Sidney Poitier says that as he looks back in life he believes in a God when he is *"pressed to the wall."* He says that most things in life, for him, fit nicely into what he calls 'Judeo-Christian ethics'.

To Poitier, it is nature, which makes most sense of his God. Our busy-ness often gets in our way, he says, and we must always fight distractions.

Is God really reliable? Though some will never agree, many good and 'important' people along with me (not that I am good or important to most people) answer with a resounding, *"Yes!"*

To me to be a true Christian takes guts. There is no weakness about it!

I am now in the twilight of my life. Though I still think I have a few unfinished chores here, I am faced, like all people and everything, with moving on. I am not afraid to move forward, but sure don't relish saying goodbye for a time to those I love. The thought of moving on causes me to reflect on two comforting passages in my scriptures. *"For I am in a strait betwixt two, having a desire to depart, and to be with Christ: which is far better (it must be nice when you love others here as much as I do): Nevertheless to abide in the flesh is more needful for you"* (Philippians 1:23-24) and *"For though I be absent in the flesh, yet am I with you in the spirit, joying and beholding your order, and the steadfastness of your faith in Christ"* (Colossians 2:5).

And do you know what? The more I learn the more I realize I don't know much and my present sickness has me rather naked and helpless in this old world.

I've come to the realization that all people, myself included, are pitiful and we all need to stop pretending otherwise. Xenophanes of Colophone was perhaps the first pre-Socratic philosopher who recognized that all human beings are flawed and that man should not venerate humans too much.

It's okay if we are concerned about our condition, but try not to panic - keeping ingrained in your mind mankind's pitifulness before God.

Life is tough. Hopelessness is always trying to push its way in. Set yourself some goals. As long as we have life, there is hope so keep going no matter what!

"Man is like to vanity: his days are as a shadow that passeth away" (Psalm 144:4) *and "...happy is that people (person), whose God is the Lord"* (Psalm 144:15, word added).

A few years ago, while running a marathon in Nashville, Tennessee, I noticed that many participants were dressed as this world's famous singers. It was then I realized once again how crazy this world and we people can be. People all too often seem to believe that Elvis is still alive and that it is God who is dead!

I believe that if a person will let Him, God will best be revealed to him/her through their struggles.

God gives us struggles as Jesus Christ Himself had to suffer to become perfected. It may sound a bit patronizing, but you are becoming someone incredible and by enduring well your suffering you will become more God-like.

God doesn't simply want us to blindly endure our suffering. He wants us to know that even difficulties and pain have their purposes. We do not accept God or our challenges because we're blind. We accept because we now can see.

I see even more clearly that our choice in mortality is God or nothing. Without Christ to me nothing makes any sense. Patiently enduring suffering makes us 'real'. No one goes looking for struggles, but in a way suffering gives us a new and more meaningful life.

To me, our real sources of 'healing' come from several bits of knowledge. First, please realize that despite your challenges, God loves you. You are His and are never really completely alone. You are His child – literally!

Doctors can help you some, but often the best they do is mask our pains. Real power lies in accepting who you are and that you are entirely without need except for Godliness!

Sometimes the real tough thing to accept is that sometimes God seems not to intervene. If your suffering continues – trust God – accept that what is, is best.

Could it be that, like the ancient Roman stoics believed, it is true? That though some might think the ultimate state of life is health and wealth, the truly good must be good at all times and in all situations – even suffering!

You may not agree with all I have said, but I know I have at least made you think. And, who knows but what you might even implement one idea and make your world just a bit easier place to live for yourself or someone else! After all, that is the best we can do while we're here.

Recently, our rural, farming town has been experiencing the effects of a drought. My religious leaders asked many church going people to fast (go without food and water for the day). We did and rain has come, but it was too late for most crops. I learned from this that fasting and prayer is not always answered just as we wish, but I believe all prayers are heard. Don't forget that with the rain comes the mud too!

What one believes matters!

In Mexico there is a volcano into which native Mexicans used to throw innocent, virtuous people to please the gods – or so they thought. Spanish conquers later believed that the devil himself lived in this same volcano. What a people believed made all the difference in how they acted.

My belief is like the Apostle Paul's. It is that people can become God-like. *"Let this mind be in you, which was also in Christ Jesus: Who, being in the form of God, thought it not robbery to be equal with God"* (Philippians 2:5,6).

Growth requires some struggling.

Really good religion is more about caring and kindness than any doctrine. Christ said, *" For I was an hungered, and ye gave me meat: I was thirsty, and ye gave me drink: I was a stranger, and ye took me in: Naked, and ye clothed me: I was sick, and ye visited me. . . . inasmuch as ye have done it unto one of these the least of my brethren, ye have done it unto me"* (Matthew 25:35,36,40).

Useful religion requires effort and it must answer the tough questions too. Where did I come from? Why am I here? Where do I go upon my death? Why is life so full of suffering? Useful theology explains life including a lack of miracles.

It is not enough for a few in this world to represent God and give us an explanation - to make sense of life for us. Everyday struggling people, of all faiths, must be able to make some sense of this painful life themselves.

I believe we can hurt a lot and still carry on. There are times we just have to let go and trust in God. What I know for sure is that God is love – always (1 John 4:16)!

God loves you and me, and one day we'll meet Him – all of us! God does not make mortality pain-free because He loves us.

I believe that even before we came to this earth, we knew we could take some struggles and strikeouts - even more than we may have thought possible.

Our bodies deserve care, but one day we'll decay. It is our spirit that never dies. We're wise when we nurture and feed both.

I liked to climb mountains and go tenting. Like our bodies, tents are temporary dwellings. I used to teach youth that our bodies are like a glove. It is the hidden fingers inside that make a glove move.

Maybe your 'glove' has a hole or two in it. No matter, because Christ once had his own body and even He had to lay it down for a while. Christ had visible wounds (holes) in His mangled body. However, because He arose, and because He promises **all** a resurrection (reuniting body to spirit) we can always take hope! I believe that healing culminates as we admit our own nothingness, really trust in God, and graciously accept His gifts!

We must eventually accept His invitation to, *"Come unto me, all ye that labour and are heavy ladened, and I will give you rest. Take my yoke (oxen once used these) upon you... and I (Christ) will give you rest... learn of me... For my yoke is easy, and my burden is light"* (Matthew 11:28-30).

There are many ways we can receive comfort as we suffer, but I believe that thinking of all He endured can help us the most – you're not alone in your challenges! Again, I am convinced that He makes mortality; with all its pain bearable and one day it will be more than fair.

Like Martin Luther King, I too have a dream. I dream of God's arms constantly outstretched towards me. I dream of a time when there will be no rich or poor, no sick, no loneliness. Yes, I dream of the time when Christ Himself will come with, *"healing in His wings"*, as promised, to this old, suffering earth again. Then there will be no aged or unfairness of any kind! And, I dream of the day when all we have experienced, all we have learned, and all we have suffered to learn along with the most meaningful mortal relationships will be ours.

Our Bibles say of Christ, *"Though he were a son, yet learned he by obedience by the things which he suffered; And being made perfect, he became the author of eternal salvation unto all them that obey him"* (Hebrews 5:8,9).

Remember, it is okay to feel sorry for yourself now and then – we're only human, but when you're done, please flush!

Perhaps you feel that you have reached the end of the rope – that your obstacles can no longer be endured. My mom says that's the time you, *"Tie a knot in the end of your rope and hang on."* In the words of a good friend of mine who has had and currently has his own struggles and strikeouts, *"That's the time you bring out the big artillery – hope!"*

I already know which team will win the World Series. It's the team with the best pitching.

Soon it will be Remembrance (Armistice) Day when I pause to remember those who traded life for my liberty - a life of peace, safety, and ease - to preserve my freedom.

You may presently be in the midst of your own private battle. Truly great individuals face their opponents head on. Be courageous as you fight your own war and enlist Christ! With Him on your side, in the end, you will always win!

I mentioned earlier about Marcus Aurelius. He walked this earth as a Roman Emperor at about 150 A.D. 'They' say he was most concerned for the poor, the slaves, and the otherwise afflicted of his time. I feel that being concerned for others and doing something to make their life easier is the best we can do in this life.

In this world if things are ever to be entirely fair – if everyone is to win – we must give more and care more – this is the bottom line in baseball and in life too! Though it has been said many times, many ways, circumstances have little power over the 'real' you unless you so allow. You then are truly free!

I had an epiphany as I wrote this book. I now more deeply realize that though life is sometimes staggeringly painful, troubles bring with them a whole new level to the meaningfulness of life.

Our aches and pains are all a result of this mortality we once chose! The time will come when Jesus Christ will personally live on this earth and when He does, as previously mentioned… *"…God shall wipe away all tears from their eyes; and there shall be no more death, neither sorrow, nor crying"* (Revelation 21:4).

This will be a tender moment. Not just anybody gets to wipe my tears. I'm counting on this 'Kleenex box' moment. You too?

In a Little League Baseball game there are usually six innings of play. In life, if we think like God, the truth is we are away from Him just a pittance of time.

No matter what struggles you may encounter during your life, remember, life is a book, which never ends!

So, until now you thought, *"Life's not fair with all its attendant struggles & strikeouts – you're right! But, it will be more than fair if we just carry on!"*

A favorite verse of my mother's goes like this. The German poet and writer, Goethe, supposedly wrote these words more than one hundred years ago. I don't mean to trivialize your trials but…

What Of That?

Tired? Well, what of that?
Didst fancy life was spent on beds of ease
Fluttering the rose leaves scattered by the breeze?

Lonely? Well, what of that?
Someone must be lonely.
Tis not given to all to feel a heart responsive, rise and fall.
To blend another life into your own.
Work may be done in loneliness; work on.

Dark? Well, what of that?
Didst fondly dream sun would never set, the sphere to loose thy
way?
Take courage yet,
Learn thou to walk by faith and not by sight,
Thy steps will guided be, and guided right.

Hard? Well, what of that?
Didst fancy life on summer holiday with lessons none to learn,
and naught but play?

Go, get thee to thy task.
Conquer or die, it must be learned.
Learn it then patiently.

No help? Nay, tis not so.
Though human help be far, thy God is nigh.
He feeds the ravens, hears His children's cries.
He's near thee wheresoere thy footsteps roam
And He will guide thee, help thee home.

It is presumptuous of me, indeed, to feel I can add to the inspired words of Goethe, yet, if I were to add one line especially for our day and certainly not to be insensitive to your individual pain and heart ache, I would simply say...

Life's not fair? Well, what of that?

And then there is this anonymously written poem that I love, which is appropriate for all pains.

God, make me brave for life, oh braver than this.
Let me straighten after pain, as a tree straightens after the rain, shiny and lovely again.

God, make me brave for life, much braver than this.
As the blown, prairie grass lifts, let me rise from sorrow with quiet eyes, knowing thy way is wise.

God, make me brave; life brings such blinding things.
Help me to keep my sight, help me to see aright. That out of dark comes light.

Life is definitely not for sissies!
A while ago a lesson I shall never forget was given at church. Apparently, a person was planning a trip somewhere – we will say Italy. This tourist, while in Italy, was planning to see the forum, the Coliseum, Michelangelo's statue of David, and more. Imagine the surprise while when deplaning the captain said, *"Welcome to Holland."*

"Holland? I wasn't thinking I'd be going to Holland!" the passenger said to himself/herself.

Stunned, the tourist asked the air attendant, *"Are we really in Holland?"*

The answer was, *"Yes. There are some beautiful things in Holland too. So, don't miss the beauty here because of your worrying about Italy."*

Such is life! When our brief time on this diamond has come to the end – when our ninth inning has ended it will be our family and our faith that made time here worthwhile and it is in remembering God in every situation (even in pain) that we find ourselves and truly discover that we are children of God.

If you allow a trial to move you nearer to your God, is it a trial or a well-disguised blessing? Think about that!

The best and perhaps the most humbling lesson a person can learn is that this world will carry on even when we're gone. We, even the most famous people, never were in charge of much! Relax! All we really need are a few kind people (a friend just dropped off cinnamon buns - hot ones at that) to help us along and we must learn to see that there is still much beauty and good around us.

Oh yes, and though we've discussed some pretty serious life-topics here, never forget to notice the humor around you. Remember how funny the word 'boogers' once was and then there was that time your classmate (or maybe it was you) passed some serious gas at a key time in a former teacher's lesson!

If these writings have helped you deal with your own suffering, because I make no personal profit from the sale of this book, perhaps I can suggest you give a book to a suffering friend. Anyone who believes in Christ and the Bible will most certainly understand my words, too.

All too often, when things go 'awry' in our life, I'm afraid people are inclined to simply feel sorry for themselves.

The truth is that even your own life is only worthwhile because of its benefit in the lives of others.

Remember, we'd all do well to give and help each other even more! And never forget that many good people have walked our suffering pathways prior to our journey. In the words of a favorite song of my father's, "**Carry on, carry on, carry on!**"

Do you understand why I like baseball so much? It's because I know of no other game where you get high-fived being put out (usually by a **sacrifice** bunt or long fly) and the whole game, like life, is about one thing – **getting home again safely!** Until that perfect day may God bless you and may we all endure our struggles well!

The final word goes to baseball. They say you can't go back in time. I choose to disagree. All I need to do in order to make some sense of today and yesterday is to sit somewhere on a beautiful summer day, eat a hotdog and some Cracker Jacks, listen to the sound of the bat, or smell a well Neats Foot oiled leather baseball glove.

Love Burns

Post Epilogue

Seems I always want one last word. Through suffering and active caring one can truly become liberated. It is only by our suffering that we can overcome all fear and all cares of this world.

In baseball I would never give up. In life let's do similarly.

I have never professed to have much wisdom, but the Christian world generally agrees that Solomon, King David's son, was wise. I think the very last words go to this great observer of life (I'm pretty sure Solomon would have loved baseball too had they played it back then).

Of suffering Solomon said, *"For in much wisdom is much grief: and he that increaseth knowledge increaseth sorrow."* (Ecclesiastes 1:18)

God bless you all in your personal struggles & strikeouts!

Burns